Lock Down Publications and Ca$h
Presents

NO TIME FOR ERROR 2

By
KEESE

Copyright © 2025 KEESE
No Time For Error 2

All rights reserved. No part of this book may be reproduced in any
form or by electronic or mechanical means, including information
storage and retrieval systems without permission in writing from the
publisher, except by a reviewer who may quote brief passages in
review.

First Edition 2025

Printed in the United States of America

This is a work of fiction. Names, characters, places, and incidents either
are products of the author's imagination or are used fictitiously. Any
similarity to actual events or locales or persons, living or dead, is
entirely coincidental.

Lock Down Publications
P.O. Box 944
Stockbridge, GA 30281
www.lockdownpublications.com

Like our page on Facebook: Lock Down Publications
www.facebook.com/lockdownpublications.ldp

Stay Connected with Us!

Text **LOCKDOWN** to 22828 to stay up-to-date with new releases, sneak peaks, contests and more…

Like our page on Facebook:
Lock Down Publications

Join Lock Down Publications/The New Era Reading Group

Visit our website:
www.lockdownpublications.com

Follow us on Instagram:
Lock Down Publications

Email Us: We want to hear from you!

Praises for *No Time For Error*

Marquis McKenzie is the Jay-Z of the book game, top five dead or alive.

-BUNN-

Marquis should change his career from writing books to writing movie scripts. He has the ability to take you from reading a book to watching a movie.

-Jade Parrish-

Marquis is making a statement with *No Time For Error*. He is taking book writing to another level. 2024 is his! Book writers step ya game up!!!

-Tyshineak Stewart

"No Time for Error" . . . that straight off da curb street life."

Dedication

This book is dedicated to both sides of the same coin. To two arms of the same body. A dedication to two separate worlds of the same city. The West end and the South side of Durham! Stop immaturely beefing and put y'all minds and bread together and get real money! Y'all both have been trying to get them 1's, now it's time to get them M's!!

Messiah? Omega? My G's, you both have the power to make such a vision a reality. Now let's "Get . . . Get . . . Get it!

Chapter 1

"You either give it to me or give it to God."
-Unknown-

It was a wintry night in Chapel Hill, North Carolina, in February, and for the first five minutes of the first half at the Dean Dome Center, the North Carolina Tar Heels were down ten points. Malik had missed a total of nine shots. Facing and adverse opponent, he found it very difficult to concentrate on dribbling and making shots, which held his team at a twenty-one-point deficit at the end of the first half against their cross-town rivals—The Duke Blue Devils.

"For crying out loud, you're dribbling the ball like its coated with oil," Roy Williams stated, chastening Malik in the locker room concerning his careless performance. "The best offense is great defense. We gotta put maximum pressure on our competitors in the second half. I know you are under a lot of pressure, being it's our rivals, but if we plan on winning this game tonight, we must play much harder than our competitors," he advised.

At the start of the second half, Malik came out with a spirit of eagerness, waving his hands, energizing the crowd of fans who had come out just to see him in action. The crowd went wild, stomping, screaming, and clapping. The noise at the Smith Center was extremely earsplitting. As soon as the ball was inbound, within the first twelve minutes of the second half, Malik put together one of the all-time best statistical games in the history of college basketball with averages of 22.2 points, 8.5 rebounds, 6.6 assists, nearly three steals, and more than one blocked shot, while shooting fifty-four percent from the floor. Malik Carter was building an MVP resume that will be hard to match, no matter what seed the Tar Heels enter the NCAA.

Malik sprinted back down court after exploding towards the rim for a violent dunk and set back up in a defensive stance when he thought he heard Jade's voice call his name from the stands. However, he knew she didn't attend the game and willed the thought from his mind. Although he felt troubled for turning down her offer to extort Ceelo with Snatch and Castro, his alter-ego began controlling his thoughts incredibly. "Bruh, it's time we moved out. You out there missing lay-ups and shit."

Unable to understand how he had missed such an easy lay-up himself, he pondered his options now even more while in the midst of crossing half court, and the more he thought about walking away from the dope game to pursue his dreams in the NBA, the more it actually bothered him consciously. Desperately trying to will such thoughts from his mind, he was shocked at the fact that no matter how hard he wanted to, he couldn't resist the vision Young Money had presented before him. Basketball suddenly became a hustle he had no desire to entertain any longer.

As he quickly dribbled through a fierce crowd of scrambling contenders, trying to prevent him from scoring, with unseen and stealth accuracy, he passed the ball behind his back with his left hand to the right of him, foreseeing the play before it unfolded. His teammate caught the ball and quickly tossed it towards the rim without hesitation for a moment.

"Ahhh!" Malik yelled, springing from the foul line, sailing towards the basket with an outstretched hand, grabbing the ball with an open palm, slamming it home with such force he rattled the goal post, knowing it was his last basket in college basketball. The arena went into an eruption;

camera phones began flashing from all directions. Roy Williams, the staff, players, and fans worldwide jumped to their feet, screaming erratically, elated with joy and high spirits. Having made his decision, Malik stripped off his jersey and flung it into the stands as he walked over to the courtside seats, approaching the CEO of the Brooklyn Nets.

"Mr. Yomar, I'm turning down your offer of entering the 2012 draft. I've been offered a much better deal in a game that needs my presence full-time," he politely replied, knowing the game he was about to give 100% to held no rules whatsoever.

Meanwhile, somewhere in a non-descript house in nearby Wake Forest, Ceelo removed his mobile from his waist and dialed a series of numbers, as he awaited the call to be answered. He glanced down at his Ulysse Nardin timepiece wondering why Jade, Trigger, and Lucky had not shown up yet. His call went straight to voicemail. Moments later, he called back.

"Yeah," a soft voice replied

"Oh, you aint try'na see what I want?"

"Do you know what time is?" she asked in a soft-spoken way, feeling on the verge of becoming a real disrespectful bitch.

"Yeah, but—"

"Then act like it," she yelled in a bitchy tone.

"Look!" he responded, refusing to give into her negative response. "I can't leave until my people gets here."

"Umm-hmm, whatever," she murmured. "Look, Carlos Carter," she began snobbishly. "It's late, I'm horny, you ain't here and I ain't in the mood right now for no more of your midnight lies."

"Ummm-hmmm. What's all this attitude 'bout?" he asked.

She grew fed up with concealing the fact she knew about his infidelity and decided to confront him about it. "How long did you think you could fuck around with my friend before I found out about it?" she bitched. "And you have the nerve to ask me, what's all the attitude about? . . . Well, just so you know, I'm no longer playing the role of one of your dumb bitches. I just thought you should know that . . . you been exposed, Boo-Boo."

Without warning, Ceelo's mind suddenly became a whirlwind of confusion, as he could not figure out how she possibly knew about his involvement with Destiny. *Did Destiny expose our sexual relationship?* he questioned himself and was at a loss of words with no explanations.

"I rest my case," Joel stated, pulling him from his thoughts. "Plead yours."

"Ma, not tonight. I got too much other shit going on to be arguing with you 'bout some bullshit. Besides, I'm tired."

"Excuse me . . . bullshit. Oh, it would be some bullshit to you since your bullshit done been exposed."

"Joel, if this all you got to talk 'bout, I'm 'bout to hang up. I told cha I'm tired."

"Boy, bye . . . if you were so tired, you'd bring your tired ass home—"

"I got shit to handle—"

"With who? Destiny?"

There was silence as he searched for the right words to express his truest love to her.

"The one you took to Quebec, the same bitch you brought a condo and Aston Martin," she yelled through the phone. "That's what you been so busy handling for some time now."

Hearing the uneasiness in her voice told him that she felt emotionally insulted and on the verge of brimming with tears.

"Joel, I know you mad upset 'bout all of this but—"

"No matter how you put it, it ain't right," she stated before bursting into tears. "She's my best friend, Ceelo."

"You're one hundred percent right but what's done is done. We can't allow what happened in the past determine our destiny or influence our future together. I just went and copped us a multi-million-dollar house out in Miami. After I do what I do we out."

"A multi-million-dollar home out in Miami, and you now telling me this? Boy, bye."

"That's only because I wanted to surprise you. As a matter of fact, we flying south this weekend. I just copped two tickets to see LeBron and Wade courtside, ya dig?"

"Let me get this clear . . . so you basically saying once this supposedly plate of fish land and get distributed, we leaving North Carolina to start a family?"

"If that's what you want. I done had a good run out here. It's time I maximized my potential before I end up in a casket or some federal penitentiary."

"Well, it does make sense, but do you honestly expect me to believe all the other shit about us starting a family?'

"You should because you know me."

"You got good intentions but you still full of shit."

"Full of shit, Joel. Even though I do what I do, I can't imagine life without you."

"Miss me with that romance shit. I haven't seen you in seventy-two hours."

"That's because I been to on Harlem shit, but wherever I go we go. I'm about there, just hold on baby."

"You keep making all these promises about what you got planned for us, but tomorrow ain't promised to none of us. You'll be lucky if you make it through the night. You need to come home, Ceelo. I got a bad feeling."

"A bad feeling? Ain't shit gone happen to me . . . why would you even say some shit like that?"

"Because something 'bout this conversation doesn't feel normal," she replied, feeling some type of way.

"What's so different 'bout this conversation than any other that we've had before now?"

"I don't know, Cee, just come home. If you love me, you'll stop whatever you're doing and come home now."

"Ma, I do love you but I can't move right now."

"I don't believe you. Regardless of what you say or how you say it, the reality of you and that bitch will forever be on my mind."

"Ma, shit ain't that serious between us. It's more business than pleasure, whether you whether you want to believe it or not."

"Oh my fucking god. No, you didn't."

"What? You think I'm just saying shit to be saying it? Ma, if I wanted to take it to that level with her, I could have taken it there easily. Your friend been on me since the day you introduced us."

"And you just now decided to tell me this shit? So basically you just sat back and watch that bitch befriend me so she could get close to you? You wack."

"Why you keep going on and on 'bout dis shit? I keep telling you it's nothing. Yeah, I slipped a few times, but our business relationship is what matters most. Anything outside of that was a temporary fix."

Joel was speechless for a moment, finding it difficult to respond. She could not believe Ceelo was spitting such elementary game in her ear. But as see-through as it sounded, Joel was beginning to slump into his trap.

"Alright, whatever! I'm willing to put whatever you got going on behind us and get from where we are to where we supposed to be in life together."

"I'm glad you finally see the bigger picture," he said, smiling to himself.

"They say big dreams attract big people . . . but let's see if you can accept and visualize this. While you were out blessing her sex kitten, Castro was gently blessing mine, and I enjoyed every inch of it. Damn! Karma is a bitch, isn't she?"

Startled by her remark, Ceelo dropped his bottle of Hennessy into his lap. "Fuck," he yelled into the receiver, bolting from the couch with a soaked lap.

"But don't sweat it, Boo-Boo, it was more business than pleasure. He only seduced me once," she said curtly, giving him a taste of his own medicine. He stood dumbfounded with nothing to say as Joel knew what she had just revealed to him blew his mind.

"Boo-Boo, you still there?" she asked.

"So that your way of getting back at me, by creeping with the help?" he responded.

"I'd expect you say some shit like that," she said.

"Look, Joel, it is what it is. Regardless of what you did or who you did it with, my love for you is endless. I just want to put this shit behind us and move forward," he confessed in a gentle way.

"Once upon a time I believed you, but now when you confessed your love to me, it had no substance whatsoever. True love requires the presence of trust. And from your actions, I don't think you possess that quality, although I pray that I'm wrong."

"Ma, regardless of what I may have done in the past, you and I are perfect for each other, but in order for us to win you gotta do away with your insecurities in order to understand why I move the way I move in them streets. Only then will you be able to fully trust me with a peace of mind."

"Insecurities indeed!" She challenged, "How can you use such a word when I'm just a pit stop in your life? I don't trust you anymore, Ceelo, and until I detect the reality of faithfulness in your action, I won't be able to take you seriously, Boo-Boo."

"Why? Cause of my devotion to the streets? I go hard the way I do so we can live comfortably, but at the end of the day you are my main focus. When you happy, I'm happy. When you sad, I'm sad. My fate is entwined with yours. What more can I say? This is what makes my life so exciting, so meaningful and fulfilling." Although his dialect sounded as though it was script, it made sense, earning her undivided attention.

"So, Destiny was just a fling and nothing more?" she asked, contemplating on forgiving him, although she knew she'd never forget.

"Basically," he assured her.

"I don't believe you," she said softly.

"I thought we agreed to put this behind us."

"We did, but it's not gonna happen overnight," she said, sounding unsure.

"Joel, you know I love you, right?"

"All I hear is empty words with no actions."

"Miss me with that. If I didn't love, you why would I trust you so completely?'

There was a brief moment of silence. However, Ceelo could not see her facial expression and felt assured they had amended their relationship. He then altered his train of thought as he heard: "Can't Raise a Man" by K. Michelle, whispering melodically through the speaker of the phone. Apparently, Joel had inserted the CD into her compact sound system.

"Cee!" Joel softly whispered through the receiver.

"What's good?" he answered.

"I have an exam tomorrow, so I need to get off this phone and get some rest. Just call me when you're on your way," she stated before ending the call.

Ceelo's thoughts were unclogged now, and he knew he had to make a sound decision fast or risk losing his arm candy, not to mention take the risk of being indicted or murdered. He began to wonder about the weight, being he wasn't completely satisfied. Suddenly, his thoughts were interrupted by the sound of a moving car pulling into the driveway.

"This better be them," he said as though someone else was present with him in the house to accompany him. After tossing his cell phone onto a nearby sofa, he headed in the direction of the front door. The moment he stepped onto the porch, he noticed Jade's Cherokee abruptly parked recklessly behind his Cherokee with the left-side passenger door detached. Swiftly, he jumped off the porch and sprinted toward the bullet-riddled vehicle. As he neared, he observed multiple bullet holes covering the entire Cherokee.

"What the fuck happened?" Ceelo asked nervously as Jade and Lucky exited the Jeep and raced towards the back seat.

"Son been shot," Lucky yelled, flinging the right-side door open. Trigger laid motionless across the back seat, bleeding intensely.

"Ma, watch out, we got 'em," Ceelo stated as she stepped aside. The moment they lifted him, he screamed in agony as though he had been injected with a thousand needles at one time.

"Ahh . . . fuck," he grunted as Ceelo and Lucky carried him into the house.

"Jade, unload the compartments!" Ceelo shouted over his shoulder.

Jade stood silent as she examined the Jeep, astonished by the fact they had made it out of the bullet-riddled vehicle alive. "God, thank you for sparing my life once again," she prayed silently to herself as she climbed into the Cherokee, pulled the emergency brake, hit the rear defrost button, and opened the sunroof. That disengaged the lock on the left- and right-side compartments. Still puzzled by the sight of one of the three task force agents, who resembled Destiny, exiting a second vehicle and clad in FBI attire, she watched as she skillfully drove away from the scene. The whole situation startled her. However, those thoughts were derailed when she noticed the two empty clips and shells scattered across the backseat and floorboard.

"Damn, Trigger showed no mercy," she thought to herself as she grabbed two neatly packed Louis Vuitton duffle bags from the secret compartment, which held numerous kilos of heroin, before strolling into the house.

Upon approaching her acquaintances, she observed Trigger lying on the couch, clutching his right shoulder. After making sure his wounds were not life-threatening, Jade and Lucky sprinted out to the Jeep to retrieve the additional kilos while Ceelo attended to Trigger's wounds. A few heartbeats later, they had emptied the Jeep of all its pharmaceutical products. Once inside, Jade took a deep breath before hitting the light switch to signal her confidantes that the shipment had arrived.

"What the fuck happened?" Ceelo asked Jade as she dropped the last of several duffle bags on the floor with a thud. Jade remained silent as Lucky expounded on what transpired on I-95 in full detail. She was mentally preparing herself for what was to come, knowing Castro and Snatch were positioning themselves to home invade at any moment.

No more than fifty yards away, two masked hood figures stood waiting, their thirst and malice swelling in their hearts, contemplating the task and journey they were about to embark on that would either make them millionaires or bring them to an early grave if the mission at hand did not unfold according to their plan.

Both felons circumspectly made their way through the wilderness, as the night was mute and nonviolent. Not a whisper could be heard under the canopy of the unresponsive midnight sky. The silver and dark-blue upper atmosphere slightly illuminated the inhabitants of the earth below as the two felons proceeded closer toward their journey's end.

Slightly climbing the flight of stairs, they stood motionless against the granite house, listening to the voices inside. "What the fuck you mean, he had to dead two FBI agents?" Ceelo thundered furiously.

"He had no choice," Jade said. "If he hadn't done what he did, we'd be in custody by now."

"Son, let that shit go, fam," Lucky cut in. "We got mouths to feed."

One of the felons peeped through the small window on the door, noticing Ceelo was unsettled about life issues. However, the moment he spun around to take the last duffle bag to the master bedroom, the second felon kicked the door in with a startling boom that alarmed those inside. Ceelo and his minions froze in fear before they could counter or comprehend what had materialized within a blink of an eye. The first felon brandished his AK-47. Immediately, he pulled the feathered trigger, letting off a thunderous explosion into the rafters, making fragments rain down.

"Everybody get the fuck on the floor!" he ordered in a murderous tone, as sheetrock cascaded down from the ceiling. Without a moment's spare, the second felon rushed through the door, gripping a military-issued, fully-loaded, automatic, remodified MP5 submachine gun equipped with a specialized suppressor attached to the barrel with a built-in cooling system.

Blaaw, Blaaw! The MP5 jerked back and forth against the armpit, ejecting hot, smoking shells over Lucky's shoulder.

"You got it, I want it, now run that shit," the first felon barked, aiming the AK-47 at Ceelo, who had spun around to confront his intruders. "You can either give it to me, or give it to God," he warned, tensing his finger on the trigger.

Ceelo stood frozen with the duffle gripped in his hand, looking into the felon's face, covered with a mask and blood-red paint, locking eyes with him, noticing a death warrant waiting to be served. Ceelo dropped the duffle slowly to the floor, looking over at Jade as she stood frozen with both hands in the air, as if she were a teller in a bank being robbed by two Zoo Gang members. Looking back at both felons dressed down in customer fatigue with only their eyes slightly showing through the blood-red paint and mask.

Quickly, both felons scrambled about the room with blurring speed. "On the ground!" the felon holding the AK-47 barked as he pimp-smacked Ceelo across the face, like a hoe who came short with her pimp's money. "You too, bitch," he grunted madly.

The second felon waved the MP5 back and forth on those who remained standing, providing his counterpart backup, as he pulled Ceelo's hands behind his back, snapping handcuffs in place.

"Where the fuck that work at?" the first felon chanted like a demonic chorus.

"You at the wrong spot, B," Ceelo said.

"We ain't got shit in here," he screamed. However, the felon holding the AK-47 was not having it, he knew the realness.

"B, you got two options . . . we can either take it and go, or take it in blood," the felon swore, meaning every word. There was silence as the felon walked across the living room, pulling a .44 revolver from his waist. "*Click!*" he thumbed the hammer black, slamming the cold barrel against the warm flesh of Ceelo's temple. "B, run dat or else Suffer Da Consequences," he stated. Having seen the wheel of the .44 in slow motion roll as the felon thumbed the hammer a second time, Jade looked down at Ceelo who was now lying face down on the floor, then back upwards towards the intruder. "You got one second!" he warned.

***

Outside the non-descript stash house, lurking in the shadowy darkness, Snatch and Castro sat in a parked rented, lustrous, ebony-painted Dodge Charger, smoking on a heavy-sized blunt before pursuing their victims. Noticing there were far more characters inside than expected baffled them.

"Bruh, bruh, I thought sis said there would only be three clients with her."

"I don't give a fuck who in there . . . they got it . . . I want it," Snatch responded eagerly.

"Let's take it in blood," Castro replied.

As the two murderers opened the car doors, three rapid explosive shots echoed with a sound that bespoke instant death.

"Oh shit!" Castro said, noticing the bright flashes through the window of the house. "You see that shit?"

***

"Now, if anyone else wanna die, I suggest y'all come off dem shits now!" the intruder advised, moving toward Trigger, who sat slouched on the couch, clutching his shoulder. He then turned onto his side in agony and screamed as the lead felon grunted, stabbing his gloved finger into the wound in Trigger's shoulder.

Trigger, wishing he had his ratchet, swore he could at least get one shot off. Jade glanced down at Ceelo, who had blood leaking from his eyes, knowing all that had transpired was not part of the script. Therefore, she could not figure out why the two felons had taken it to such extremes. She knew she had to make a decision quickly, being they were on their Red Rum, fearing she would be killed next.

"Okay, okay!" she shouted. "I know where everything is, just don't take my life."

"Cuff those two," the lead felon ordered his counterpart. Within a matter of seconds, he had both clients cuffed together. Both felons then dragged Jade into the master bedroom. Once inside, they frantically began searching the slightly furnished room. The lead intruder opened the walk-in closet and stepped inside.

"Money!" he barked, loud enough for his counterpart to hear.

The lead intruder stood amazed by what sat before him in a mini-safe with the door slightly open. In front of the safe sat Louis Vuitton duffels with individually wrapped kilos of heroin concealed in each duffel. He quickly pulled the duffels from the safe, loading the kilos into separate bulletproof duffels that sat nearby. After emptying the contents of the duffels and safe, he zipped both duffels—filled with money and heroin—and flung one of the duffels to his confidant, then flung the other over his shoulder. Both felons hurriedly ran through the house and exited just as they had come, backtracking through the woods, headed for the rented BMW where a third party waited patiently, committed to the vision with a clear definition of purpose.

Upon reaching the vehicle, both felons removed their masks and bulletproof jackets, tossing them into the trunk with the duffel bags and AK-47. The felon with the MP5 jumped into the backseat as the supremely seductive hood diva slammed the trunk shut and slid into the front passenger seat. The lead felon smiled with loyalty as he eyed the Zoo Gang symbol that had been tattooed on the diva's neck.

"I knew you'd pull it off, daddy," the young mistress stated softly as he pulled into the midnight traffic.

"Bruh-bruh, we accomplished what we set out to accomplish," the lead intruder's second-in-command stated from the backseat. "Now we gotta focus on getting dem shits off."

"That's my least worry," the driver said.

***

Back at the non-descript stash house, Jade kneeled down to the floor, holding the head of her companion's lifeless, bloodstained body, resting in her lap. She screamed at the top of her lungs while trying to stuff the organs back into the enormous hole in Ceelo's chest. Blood covered her hands, still warm from the touch.

"It's time we bounced," Jade continuously cried as Lucky repeatedly told her that Ceelo was dead and that they needed to bounce. He then slowly helped Jade to her feet, still in a zombie state, as he then helped her into the passenger side of

Ceelo's Jeep. He rushed back inside and carried Trigger from the house into the backseat, noticing that Trigger was now conscious, as the bullet had made a clean pass through his shoulder. Time was what Jade and Lucky needed to recover from it all. Lucky thought to himself as he drove away in silence, with vengeance he'd devised in his heart for violence.

Chapter 2

"Progress Always Involves Risk"
-Malik-

The following day, two detectives showed up at Joel's estate, informing her that Ceelo had been brutally murdered, and that they thought the motive was a heist. They also informed her that the Cherokee Jeep which had been used during a federal agent homicide that left another critically wounded had been parked in the driveway of the house where Ceelo's body had been found, and the DMV records showed it had been registered to the deceased.

The detectives suspected that whoever was driving the Jeep the previous night was solely responsible for Carlos "Ceelo" Carter's death. When asked if she knew of anyone who may have committed such brutality, she responded that she did not have a clue. When asked if she knew of anyone named "Lucky," she lied, saying it was Carlos Carter's alias. She could not believe the disturbing news and took it very hard. Once the detective left, she climbed into her Vispring luxury bed and cried for hours until she fell asleep.

Somewhere deep in South Miami, while surfing through his smartphone, Castro discovered that he had several missed calls and voice messages, mostly from Joel. When he phoned her back sometime that night, he informed her that he had received her messages and the fact that he had already heard the news regarding Ceelo's death through an acquaintance. She cried the entire call until she convinced him that she did not want to be wrapped in his arms. He assured her that he would be over to console her once he and his client came to a mutual agreement. Later that night, around 10:45, his flight landed at RDU. He arrived at Joel's estate moments before she attempted to take a bottle of sleeping pills. Refusing to accept such a foolish act, he curved her but quickly dismissed the thought and, with sound decision, he comforted her with warm and embracing arms as she cried upon his shoulders.

With his street wisdom, he helped her understand that Ceelo's death was not her fault and that she needed to pull herself together, just like a well-paid-off peer counselor would advise. He could not come to a conclusion as to why she would blame herself for Ceelo's murder by any means, when, in fact, she was Ceelo's arm candy.

Days later, Joel fell into a zombie-like state of depression. She would not eat, talk to anyone, bathe, or respond to Castro's touch or leave the master bedroom. However, she managed, on Saturday night, to fly to New York to attend Ceelo's funeral the following day.

Upon seeing Jade, Snatch, Malik, Asia, Destiny, and other companions and family members of Ceelo when she and Castro arrived, it made her feel better. She was surprised at the large gathering of people who came out to pay their last respects to the fallen soldier. Due to the enormous number of people attending the service, they shut down three city blocks in Harlem.

Returning back to North Carolina with Castro, Joel slowly began to will herself back together. In a matter of forty-eight hours, she was back to normal—moving about seductively, cooking meals for Castro, smiling, laughing, eating sensibly, and jogging every morning. Castro stood by her side every step of the way and was pleased to see Joel refreshed and to her old self again.

That night, he prepared an affectionate dinner that included buffalo shrimp, cheesecake, crab legs, chicken sliders, and more while Joel settled down in the entertainment room in front of the 125-inch screen, watching The *Face Diddy* story. While chefing in the kitchen alone, peering through the oversized window, Castro saw a figure move in the rear yard near the pool. With sleekness, he pulled his cannon-sized HK-P7 that the special Greeks used from his holster and eased out the back door, around some shrubs on the patio. Spotting a figure clad in all-black fatigue, looking very much the part of a successful mercenary, now squatting beside his CL550 Benz, Castro dashed around the garage, gun in hand, and crouched to within two feet of the intruder's back. He leaned forward, placed the HK-P7 near the intruder's head, kicked him to the ground, and in a vexed tone, stated, "Who sent you?" Castro then smacked the intruder with the butt of his gun, then kicked him again as he rolled over and finally got a glimpse of his assailant. Minutes into the interrogation, the assailant revealed to Castro who had put a bounty on his head. Castro then placed his gun to the intruder's forehead and pulled the trigger.

Flit, flit! The slim-sized cannon coughed, jerking twice in his hand. Castro then dragged the lifeless body into the garage, dumping his corpse in the trunk of his Hooptie.

As he began walking towards the house, he noticed Joel standing on the patio and wondered how long she had been standing there.

"Castro, what you got going on, booboo?"

"Everything good," he stated as he walked onto the patio. "Just go in the house."

"What's all the candles around the hot tub for?" she asked, sounding perplexed.

"I wanted to do something special for you. You've been through a lot these last couple weeks," he gamed. "You deserved it, so relax," he charmed, sitting down beside her.

After rewarding him with an affectionate kiss, Castro stood and walked into the kitchen to fix their plated which he had prepared. Over dinner, they laughed and picked each other's mind while conversing. However, Castro's mind never wondered from the fact that Zulu had a bounty over his head.

He could not understand why he even considered him knowing Ceelo was Malik's connection.

Later that night, after making slow delicious love to Joel, Castro showered and smoked a weed-filled blunt before calling Jade. Briefly, he explained in detail the situation with Zulu. After ending the call, Jade rolled over and fell back to sleep in a matter of seconds after informing Castro to call her the following day.

"God nooo!" she yelled, after a recurring nightmare, reflecting back to the tragic event she had witnessed, suddenly being approached by two masked men who moved similar to US soldiers raiding a terrorist palace. One of the masked men's cocky, yet smooth swagger, kept tugging at her.

"Nooo! Nooo!" she screamed in the dark, trying to recall where she knew such swag and who owned it. Sweating under her Chanel sheets, her hands were covered with Ceelo's blood. However, she never meant for anyone to get hurt.

"Ahhh!" she screamed, a second before bolting upright in bed with her eyes wide open, breathing heavy as she finally found a way to calm herself. She then reached for her smartphone, which sat in its charger alongside the bed, and phoned Malik on his second phone that only a chosen few had the number to.

"Red Rum Salute," he answered confidently as he placed the phone to his ear.

"What's good, Papi? Red Rum Salute."

Recognizing Jade's voice, he grabbed the remote from his lap, pushed a button, and the movie on the screen went mute, filling the theater with silence.

"Not shit, just sitting here watching *Temptation*," he responded, sensing that Jade was bothered by life issues. "What's good with you?" he asked, in a caring way.

"Nothing," she whispered softly.

"You lying . . . I can hear it in your voice," he responded, glancing over at Asia as she lay motionless beside him, stretched out with her head upon his chest.

"You think you know me so well, don't you?" she laughed.

"I know you well enough to know when your spirits are low, and when you need to be held," he whispered, causing her to gasp through the phone. "You in the mood for some pillow talk?"

"Do you think it will help?" she asked, just wanting the nightmares to cease.

"Communication has always worked for me," he suggested.

"You feel like coming over?" she asked. "I'd feel much better if you were here with me."

"Really?" he asked.

"Yes, really. I've always felt safe while in your presence, and besides, I can't stop thinking about what happened to Ceelo," she confessed.

"Are you still having those nightmares?"

"Sort of, but it be more like God be trying to reveal who murdered Ceelo to me. It's sort of like a puzzle I'm trying to put together."

"Stop stressing yourself over things you have zero control over."

"You right," she stated softly.

"Have you eaten anything?"

"I had a salad earlier, but all I did was pick on it."

"A'ight, give me a few minutes. I'll be over as soon as I feed Cain and Abel." He was referring to the two Rottweilers he always left in the house for Asia's protection.

"Angel dust!"

"Say it two times," he said before ending the call.

Jade climbed from the bed into the shower. Moments later, she padded out of the bedroom into her connected bedroom, naked, skin damp and warm still from the shower. Never in a rush to put on clothes, the ringing of her cell phone served as a perfect distraction and excuse to remain naked a little while longer. She frowned as she saw the screen but still answered it. There was no reply, so she disconnected the call. "Who the fuck keep playing on the phone?" she questioned herself as she sat on the plush leather sofa, thinking how Ceelo's murder might haunt her for the rest of her life like a scary movie.

Although the hottest commodity to ever roam through the streets of Durham, Jade lacked the most significant quality of the mental law . . . how to eliminate self-defeating thoughts and habits. She persistently allowed thoughts of Ceelo's demise to magnify in her life. She was curious to know who the two notorious murderers were responsible for Ceelo's expiration date and the hundred kilos she had routinely set out to have extorted that would have moved her and the members of her team into the playoffs. That achievement of such a goal she had routinely set would have changed their lives forever. She gave serious thought to using her confidants like pawns in a deadly game of chess that must be relied upon by the wits in order to uncover the truth. Wouldn't that be a goal worth pursuing with passion?

Suddenly her thoughts vanished like spirits unseen when the doorbell sounded. She knew Malik had his own key, so before she decided to answer the door, she slipped into her bedroom in search of her ten-thousand-dollar U-Neak designer bag. Inside sat a chrome-plated P89 favored by most female law enforcement officers.

"Who is it?" she stated as she circumspectly sauntered her way into the living room, peeking through the security hole, gripping the P89 Malik had given her by her side.

"Pizza Hut," the delivery man stated. She had smelled the pizza as she neared the door.

Pizza Hut . . . I ain't ordered no damn pizza, she thought silently. She then unbolted the front door and spoke through the chain.

"Boy, you scared the shit out of me," she gasped as she unlocked and opened the door. They exchanged warm hugs. However, Malik could tell instantly that she had many issues on her mind. She was barefoot, in some cute Agent Provocateur panties and bra, looking supremely seductive.

"Gurl, bye . . . you have been tested in these streets by far worse and have proven that you're nothing to be fucked with," he stated, marching in past her. "That's what makes your story that much more interesting," he stated as he spat the pizza box down on the coffee table, along with a brown bag containing more treats. "Look, I brought you a surprise," he smiled wickedly. "The world's finest ultra-premium tequila," he stated as he reached into the bag, removing a bottle of Patron, flashing its label.

"You're trying your best to cheer me up, ain't cha?" she stated, giving him a seductive gaze that could melt cheese.

"I'm just tryin' to make sure you good, Ma," Malik piped in on cue.

"Yeah, I'm straight, but here lately I've been finding myself sleeping less. I been having those nightmares constantly," she stated, looking out the window overlooking the night traffic.

"I can imagine what you're going through."

The moment she spun around, his eyes dropped, caressing every delicate curve on her body, revealing itself as she sauntered her way towards the kitchen. Noticing her cute pink panties, his eyes lingered longer than usual. Unconsciously, he licked his soft pink lips, unaware that she was watching him, instantly reading his mind.

"I gotta have some of that," he stated, while staring at the outline of her hips.

"Tonight?"

"Not tonight, boo-boo. This kitty on lock down, but if you can find the key, all this treasure can be yours," she stated, looking him squarely in the eyes as she sat down beside him on the love seat.

"What if I told' cha I'm holding the kitty hostage tonight?" In a strange way, his word delighted her soul.

Light-heartedly, she giggled at his humorous tone. Her breasts quivered underneath the fabric that strained to hold them in place.

"So what you been up to?" She already knew the answer to her question, but she wanted him to verbalize it in detail. "You haven't been in contact with anyone since the funeral. It's like you've fallen completely back from the team," she continued as she shut the plaza off, turning Keyshia Cole's newest CD on with a touch of the remote.

Music instantly filled the room with such clarity, it sounded as if it were an orchestra. Placing her gun on the table and shifting, folding her legs beneath her thighs, she faced him with soft eyes. Carefully, he lifted her gun from the table.

"I'm still pushing it to the limit, sun up 'til sun down. I just had to fall back for a minute and see how that situation with Ceelo unravel, 'cause those same dudes might be plotting to get at me," he replied, setting the ratchet back down. "Why you walking around the house wit'cha gun out?"

Jade shrugged. "Shit, I ain't tryin' to get caught slippin' either. Now that niggas giving out death orders, I gotta be extra on point."

Malik extended his hand to open the box at the foot of the bed. She closed her eyes and sucked in the heavy aroma of black olives, Portobello mushrooms, Italian sausage, green peppers, and six different cheeses. Jade had eaten a thousand pizzas from Pizza Hut, especially during her high school years at Hill Side High School.

"You look like death warmed over, eat up."

"Who you supposed to be, my dietitian now?" she giggled girlishly.

"Do you really want me to answer that?" he asked.

"Of couuuurssee!" she mumbled.

"You wouldn't want that, but if I was a dietitian, I would recommend that you have plenty of meat in your diet," he stated, locking eyes with hers.

Jade devoured her first slice of pizza without a word, then went for a second.

"So what's the plan now?" she asked curiously while wiping her chin with a napkin as she paced her slice back into the box. "We need a new connect," she stated while sipping from the Patron bottle.

"I found us a connect who can provide us with tons of blocks," he spoke with rapid-fire confidence. "I just gotta find a way to get it back from the Midwest."

"That sounds interesting—way more interesting than I expected," she beamed.

In Jade's safe, opulent, 1.2 million gated community condo in Raleigh, they fed each other pizza, while sipping tequila and creating a flow of ideas into each other's minds. Malik even cracked a few jokes and did impressions, deadpanning quotes from his favorite movie *American Gangster*, confiding every thought and feeling, including their affection for each other. Malik also shared with his companion that the reason he dropped out of college was because that type of game was no longer a challenge for him and the fact that he had lost excitement and interest. Asia consumed most of her time in the pages of textbooks. In so many words, he told Jade all she needed to know: how to stay committed to the vision and how to maximize their relationship.

With Malik and his alter-ego "Young Money" coming up with a definiteness of purpose to see past their present into their future for their brand and crew members, it was something they chose not to discuss with Jade because the hundred kilos he now kept in storage in one of his nondescript stash houses had to remain anonymous until the two decided to put their vision into action. Although no one knew of the home invasion other than Malik, Hysheem, and Rachel, Jade was in the blind and had no knowledge he was the one solely responsible for Ceelo's murder.

"So we on our way into the play-offs?" she asked, thinking of a way to further her own desires.

"Didn't I tell you in the first half of the season that in two years we would win a championship?" he spoke as if the non-existent had already existed.

"More or less."

"Progress always involves risk. Big-time players make big-time plays on the big stage. It's all about chemistry, Ma. When you drafted me and put the ball in my hand, I showed you how to execute in close situations down the stretch—"

"But more important, it was great to see we were able to position ourselves and get stops. That's where the game was won, and we did it. But I still think we should fall back for a while, 'cause shit's crazy hot right now. The Feds might be watching… it's a known fact they were watching Ceelo. So, what makes you think they're not watching us?"

"Why should we let anything or anyone stop us from doing what we have the ability to do? Our goal from the beginning was to win championships, so we ain't got no time to be falling back, 'cause you never know when shit might turn around."

"I only mentioned the Feds because of that situation that popped off on the highway."

"It is what it is. Consequences, whether positive or negative, are actually beneficial and always educational. We gon' be alright. You can't be afraid to win," he consulted with his timepiece, a Richard Mille, before continuing. "This series is going to have a happy ending."

"I'm with you, but you know we gotta put maximum pressure on our competitor's defense, 'cause they gon' be aiming for you, Malik."

"I already know I gotta get more aggressive, but niggas already know I bang them hammers, and I keep them blooded goons by my side at all times."

"Just be careful, Malik. We already lost one of our starters not even two weeks ago. I don't want to be responsible for anything happening to you. I would never be able to live with myself."

"Nah, you lost Ceelo. You can miss me with that touchy-feely bullshit. Just a few weeks ago, he was just a client. Look, we on our way to another level of success that I believe will satisfy all of us, but we only got one shot at this shit, Ma. It's now or never . . . ain't no sequel," he assured her.

Jade lifted her head, locking eyes with his. "Sent from Heaven" filled the room as Keyshia Cole's angelic voice penetrated their souls with strong emotions neither of them could shake off.

"Jade, you drop-dead gorgeous without trying," he said while caressing the clouds of her black curly hair with a gentle touch. "I've never been someone shy 'til I seen your eyes. I wish you could see what I see, every time I look at you." Her heart fluttered as he described the effect she had on him.

"Describe what you see when you look at me, Malik."

"I see a rose that needs to be nurtured with kindness and watered with my love."

Jade pondered his words, recalling little in particular that he had said, but rather the feeling it had given her. She tried to speak, but he silenced her. "Shhh . . ." Placing a finger to her lips slowly, he leaned toward her. As she closed her eyes, the moment their lips made contact, her breathing became heavy, and her heart rate rose from the passion she now felt.

Nothing or no one mattered at that very moment besides his kiss.

Jade slowly laid back on the couch and seductively nibbled at his ear as Malik nibbled at hers. "Ah, Malik," she sucked air between her teeth strongly. "Sssss." While arching her back toward his body, her hands found their way under his Polo sweater, rubbing his back with soft touches as the sensation of pleasure shot through her entire body, tingling every nerve within her. "Ummmm," she moaned seductively as the heat of wetness built between her thighs.

Having always fantasized about him when she was alone, now felt as satisfactory as what she was experiencing at the present moment. Frantically, she fumbled at his Polo belt until she had his sizable warm love muscle in her hand. "Oh my God!" she thought in silence, feeling its length, mass, and size. "Damn, boo-boo, you super strapped . . . ummm . . . ahh . . . maaa-aakee love to me, papi," she gasped, spreading her thighs, wrapping her legs around his waist.

"Jade, do you love me?" he said, pressing a lingering kiss on her soft, wet, sexy lips.

"Yes, fuck yeah . . . I love your mindset, ambition, and flamboyant look," she stated, pulling her panties off as fast as time would permit. Holding her breath as she felt him ease the head of his love muscle between the secret opening of her nookie.

"Owww, damn, you got that wet-wet," he stated as he slowly penetrated her soul, as music filled their minds. She drifted on a cloud of pleasurable ecstasy.

"Shit," she cursed under her breath, realizing the music she heard were the words coming from her ring-tone. Wanting to ignore it, she found she couldn't. The more she fought to restrain from answering it, the more it rung.

"Puh-leese don't answer it," Malik whispered as he slid his love muscle deeper into her second mouth. "We 'bout to lock ourselves in this condo and fuck for days," he predicted, not wanted the moment to end, realizing she had that theory.

Shifting under his weight, she extended her arm out and grabbed her phone from off the lampstand just as Keyshia Cole's smooth crooning filled the air, perfectly complementing the mood. She looked rattled; however, she answered intensely and loyally. "Hello." Suddenly, she squirmed from underneath Malik, gently moving him to the side as she slung her legs off the bed and sat up at full attention. There were a few fast moments of mumbling he couldn't quite understand. "I'm on my way . . . let me slip some jeans on," she promised, before ending the call.

"What's going on?" he questioned, zipping his thousand-dollars jeans up. Jade walked off, yelling over her shoulder as she entered the walk-in-closet.

"Carla was in an accident and had to be hospitalized. That was Monique."

"She okay?"

"Mo didn't say," she stated as she strutted back into the living room, her eyes hard as she scanned the room for her Chanel bag. "You staying here or are you coming with me?"

"I'll swing back through, just call me."

Jade looked him in the eyes, wanting to apologize because the mood had been disturbed, knowing they had waited a lengthy amount of time for that moment to finally unfold. "You good, your friend needs you," he said, letting her know he understood fully. "We'll make up for it . . . I promise," he smiled, coming up with a plan.

Chapter 3

"Welcome to the Family"
-Mr. White-

"Fam, let's bounce," Snatch yelled while posted up at the entrance of "Diamonds Are Forever," aiming a MP5 at customers and two employees, who were forced to lay face down on the marble floor, hands over their heads.

"Chill, bruh . . . I'm almost done!" Castro yelled from behind the counter as he quickly snatched the last of eight trays from their racks, dumping them into the black military-style backpack. Without a moment to spare, he zipped the bag, hopped over the counter, and threw the bag to Snatch, informing him he was headed for the vault. Snatch protested that there wasn't enough time, knowing Castro was an "Official General" at heart and would use the mastermind principle as he strived toward cleaning out the vault.

"On ya feet!" he barked, grabbing the jeweler by the collar and lifting him. "You don't belong in the U.S. no way," he stated, slapping the foreigner across the face with his S11 Executive 40-caliber handgun and shoving him into the back office.

"Give it to me or give it to God," he said, placing the ratchet behind the foreigner's ear, thumbing the hammer back. "I can either take it and go, or take it in blood," he demanded.

Kneeling before the vault, the jeweler looked around, frightened, as he started mumbling incoherently that he didn't know the combination.

"It's vital that we engage our imaginations in the process of making winning decisions," Snatch thought back on what Malik had told his entourage one night at a strip club in Miami called King of Diamonds.

When the owner resisted, Castro's gun umped: *Bloaow!* It thundered, splattering blood and fragments of the foreigner's brain against the door of the vault, like it had been airbrushed on the vault. Dashing back out front, he grabbed what seemed to be the owner's wife, shoving her to the back where the vault sat. After seeing her husband's brains scattered all over the floor, she quickly knelt before the vault, opening it. She knew any resistance would be or might lead to her death.

"That's all he had to do," he stated, pulling her away from the vault. He emptied the safe of its contents in a matter of seconds. "Let's get outta here," he yelled to his confidante as he leaped over the counter, heading for the front door like the Panthers' rookie running back Jonathan Stewart eluding the Bears' number-one defense.

Both hustlers scrambled swiftly, exiting the jewelry store just as a patrolman pulled into the parking lot, screeching to a complete stop. The moment Snatch stepped foot onto the pavement, one of the officers sprang from the vehicle, retrieved his firearm, and fired, successfully striking Snatch in the center of the chest, knocking him to the ground and making the MP5 tumble from his grip.

"I'm good, cover me," he grunted, catching his breath from the force of the slug smashing against the metal plate of the Teflon he had snatched from white boy Jeff. With the true honor of a soldier, Castro returned fire and watched as the second officer slumped over in the driver's seat. He kneeled down, seized the MP5, and tossed his confidante over his shoulder. After tucking his tool into his waist, he swiftly spun with the ratchet aimed. He held down the trigger of the remodified MP5, answering back with deadly rapid force, punching holes in the police car the size of golf balls, as the machine gun hammered back and forth against his waistline. He scrambled to the getaway car, knowing the officer couldn't possibly fire back without the risk of being shot by a hail of bullets like those that descended from the upper atmosphere.

"Bruh, you able to drive?" Castro asked Snatch, helping him into the car as bullets ripped through the vehicle. "Hand me another clip."

"Get'cha Red Rum on, Bruh-Bruh," he grunted, tossing Castro a full clip. Castro caught the magazine, knowing he had to face the consequences of his actions in order to become the ultimately successful hustler he set out to become. Expeditiously, he reloaded as a bullet whizzed by his head. "Oooohhh," he flinched, slamming the fully loaded clip against the palm of his hand, like an action figure. He raised the machine gun, returning fire as the cop ducked behind the fender, scared shitless. Bullets slammed into the car as he advanced on it in search of the patrolman.

Rounding the front bumper, he surprised the young officer as he was reloading his Glock 45. Raising his gun, Castro emptied six slugs into the officer's head and then sprayed the windshield, ensuring the driver was unresponsive. Onlookers, who had been ducking behind cars, telephone poles, and into businesses, looked on as the two masked men dressed in Desert Storm fatigues sped off, burning distinctive black rims and tires.

Upon pulling into one of the many stash houses' driveways after switching cars, the duo looked at one another, releasing a deep wheeze. Then laughter exploded among the two infamous villains.

"Bruh, you shell," Snatch said, flickering a lighter in his right hand while slowly rotating a blunt into the flame with his left.

"What'cha mean, bruh-bruh?" Castro stated seriously.

"The way you be performing onstage, bruh. You be taking shit to the extreme," he smiled, revealing a top and bottom grill with diamond cuts.

"Nah, dude tried to push the red button, on some superhero shit, so I ended his career . . . sacrifices gotta be made," he stated, exiting his Cherokee.

"I love da shit," Snatch laughed as they made their way up the brick-paver circular driveway. They entered through the Brazilian oak doors covered with artistic glass and made their way through the fine limestone flooring to the grand foyer where they usually enjoyed the most captivating views of the lake. Upon hearing movement in the driveway, both hustlers reached for their ratchets and dashed to the window, spotting a torch-red Maserati with an extremely beautiful arm candy reclined in the ebony leather passenger seat. Her Egyptian bronze skin tone, along with her mesmerizing eyes and clouds of torch-red hair, were accentuating her baby-doll face. As the driver stepped out of the car, clad in Polo with at least a hundred thousand dollars' worth of jewelry wrapping his neck and both wrists, Jay-Z's newest CD could be heard at a decent level. Momentarily, the driver stood outside of the vehicle, briefly conversing with the diversified diva, before he decided to head toward the house.

There are moments when time stops to experience beauty.

"Oh, that's Bruh and Destiny," Castro barked, admiring the flesh of the new Maserati and its distinctively sculptured profile.

"Malik, let me use your phone real quick . . . my battery just went dead," Destiny yelled from the passenger side window.

"Red Rum Salute," he stated, stepping onto the porch as Destiny waved at Snatch.

"Gurl, bye."

Since Ceelo's death, Malik and Destiny had been spending a considerable amount of time together. She had seduced him one night while out at BET's *Rip The Runway* fashion show in New York City with her alluring appearance. Malik's desire for her was so powerful that night that he gave her an unforgettable moment, then he vanished. Although she knew he dealt with a bevy of exotic celebrities and hood models, which only made him more interesting, Destiny had no interest in being an independent woman. Codependence was more her preference. It was clear that their companionship was written in the stars . . . at least, that's what she told him.

"What it do, made men?" Malik bellowed as he stepped through the Brazilian oak doors onto the limestone flooring.

"You already know . . . tryna come up and add a couple stacks to my pockets," Castro said, pointing to the diamonds and custom-made jewelry scattered about the table, like a jewelry store on display.

"How much do you think this shit worth?" Malik asked, retrieving a platinum ring with a gargantuan yellow stone on it.

Castro examined the ring as if he were an experienced jeweler, just as his father had taught him over the many years.

"Bout a hunnit-an-twenty bands," he answered back.

"You bullshitting, right?" Snatch cut in.

"Hell nah, shit, I might be a couple bands off," Castro smiled, holding the ring up toward the ceiling. "Look at the clarity," he added.

"So, give me an estimate on everything," Malik stated.

Taking a moment to think, Castro studied the diamonds and custom-made jewelry displayed on the table, then whistled like a man on a construction site, eyeing an exotic hood diva strolling by. "Anywhere from 1.5 to two million. We came off this time."

Snatch smiled, wanting to know how Castro was gonna fence off two million dollars' worth of jewelry without the Federal Bureau's involvement. Malik took a seat as Castro explained the situation in full detail. When he finished giving his confidants the full layout, Malik seized the opportunity to purchase a gift for one of his vixens.

"Bruh, what's the tag team on them rings?" Malik asked, standing to his feet, facing Castro.

"Which one, bruh-bruh?" Castro stated, trying to figure out which ring Malik was interested in.

"The pink one . . . I'll give you ten bands for it right now."

After a few seconds of examining the pink sapphire, Castro agreed because the ring was only priced at sixty thousand. After they made the exchange, Malik informed both crooks he would link back up with them later before casually returning to the world's most beautiful sports car, where his companion awaited him.

Castro and Snatch both gathered their personal tote bags and headed for their separate Jeeps after they had exchanged their attire.

"Bruh, I'll swing back through wit' your cut later. Ah-ight?" Castro barked to Snatch over the hood of the Jeep as he climbed in. "Where you gone be? Out here or at your B.M.'s?"

"Just hit me . . . ain't no telling where I'll be. Angel Dust."

"Say it two times," Castro stated before pulling off, headed in opposite directions from his counterpart.

Hours later after Castro had conducted business with one of his personal clients that he didn't want his inner circles to know about, he coasted in his father's driveway. Parking behind a '68 Corvette, '70 Chevelle, a Rolls Royce Ghost, and a convertible Aston Martin, he sat for a few seconds in silence, then killed the engine, admiring the exceptionally clean vehicles. He then opened the driver-side door, slid out from behind the wheel, grabbed his duffle bag that held the remaining pieces of diamonds and jewelry, and donned a pair of Chanel shades, smiling as he walked into the house. He knew he had already made a quick eighty thousand selling a few pieces to Messiah and was only a couple of steps away from making a more powerful move with one of his father's connects.

"Glad you could make it, my son," Ervin stated, greeting him as he walked into the den. "For a minute, I thought you might not make it after watching the six o'clock news," he added in a calm way.

"Nah, everything's good; I just got caught up in another meeting with a client that didn't end too well," he expressed, as though he were a legitimate businessman.

"So, you're all squared away now?" his father asked, dressed sharply in his Ermenegildo sports coat with the matching pants and pin-striped shirt.

"At least for now, I am," he responded. "I don't see any problems that would prevent us from doing any future business together."

Mr. Wallace stared at his son a moment before speaking, admiring his style and well-spoken manners in the company of a billionaire. He was highly impressed by the expensive attire his son had chosen for the occasion. Clad in a wool double-breasted coat, a cashmere three-button, three-piece suit, a cotton dress shirt, and a silk tie—all made by Tom Ford—he looked the part. On his wrist sat a timepiece designed by David Yurman, flooded in red diamonds.

"You ah-ight, pops?"

"Yeah, everything's fine, I'm just admiring your attire," he responded. "You gon' have to introduce me to your stylist one day," he joked, and lighthearted laughter erupted in the room. "Castro, I'd like for you to meet a very dear friend of mine . . . Mr. White," he said, gesturing toward Mr. White, who sat on his left. "Mr. White . . . this is my son, Castro," he continued, as they shook hands. "Mr. White and I have been doing business together for many years, my son, way before you were even thought of."

"You two invested in a car lot together. I remember the stories you used to tell me about."

Suddenly, both men exploded in laughter, looking at him as they shared a personal joke Castro had no knowledge of. He was clueless that the car dealership was only a front to smuggle kilos of heroin and diamonds from one state to the next.

"Let's take this meeting into my office. Mr. White wants to enlighten you on a few business ventures," Ervin informed him. Castro was now skeptical and gave Mr. White the once-over. The man was much older than his father, with salty white hair, a nicely trimmed beard, and a Stefano suit, which was much more expensive than the one his father and he wore.

Giving the man a head nod, they stepped into Mr. Wallace's office, grabbing a seat around the plush leather couch.

"Castro, do you have the merchandise?" Mr. White asked, wasting no time. Lifting the duffle bag, Castro placed it on the table and unzipped it, allowing Mr. White to glance inside. Mr. White reached into his coat pocket, removing a small black eye lens to examine the diamonds one by one, as Castro and his father looked on, admiring his professionalism in silence.

"Castro, your father has shared with me all you've accomplished in your career and how extremely talented you are. And as a businessman, I had to meet such a gifted young man like yourself in person," he stated, carefully choosing his words as he continued to inspect the diamonds.

Upon finishing the inspection, Mr. White explained other business ventures he and Castro's father had engaged in over the years. He then reached between his legs, retrieving a briefcase, placing it on the table. He opened it and spun it around for Castro to examine its contents.

Bolting to his feet, Castro's eyes took on a cheerful glow as he stood, shocked by the amount of capital neatly wrapped before him. Instantly, he envisioned himself, Joel, and his confidants spending lavishly with more kilos of heroin than a Cuban caught red-handed on a cargo ship out at sea.

"Castro, that's a quarter million for the diamonds and an additional hundred thousand for your trouble with law enforcement."

"That's an extremely large amount of bread for my troubles, Mr. White," Castro stated calmly.

Noticing Castro's body language appeared more elated than he had expected, Mr. White decided to let the young hustler enjoy a few moments before revealing his main purpose for their first business encounter.

"Here's another hundred and fifty thousand in advance for another job I'd like for you to accompany with a few dolls from my mastermind alliance." Castro turned to his father, who nodded his head in agreement, indicating that it was official. "If that's not enough . . .," Mr. White paused, "Then I can arrange to have more delivered to you."

"There's no need. What's been offered is reasonable . . . I'm in," he responded, knowing it would take at least two months to make that kind of money in the streets due to the recession. "What is it exactly you need me to do, Mr. White?" he asked, while sipping on a glass of Le'ona Tequila priced at eight hundred dollars a bottle.

Briefly, Mr. White filled Castro in on the details, revealing that he had a team of diversified divas who specialized in jewelry theft and would be joining him on the project—the largest wholesaler in the Dallas Diamond District. He explained the security, escape route, and everything that was required, which sounded like a scene from the movie Ocean's Eleven.

"Last chance . . . are you satisfied?" he asked Castro, who nodded a third time. "There will be another in-depth briefing before the actual take," he assured him. "I'll send for you two days prior, which should be enough time for you to get acquainted with the others . . . welcome to the family," he smiled, satisfied.

After tossing the money-filled briefcase into the back seat, Castro sat behind the wheel, envisioning his future endeavors. He glared out the window, admiring the most dynamic Rolls-Royce in history, owned by Mr. White, visualizing Joel and himself casually navigating in and out of traffic, living a wealthy and content lifestyle. Constantly, he wondered how much the Ghost had cost. Suddenly, he laughed out loud the moment he glanced down at the license plate, which read "2 Much-4-U, Miami, FL."

Chapter 4

"Consequences Are Actually Beneficial"
-Malik-

It was cold and dreary when Castro pulled into the hewn iron gates and lush hedges on the most prestigious lane somewhere in RDU's most desirable area, with breathtaking views of downtown Raleigh. Upon entering the estate, duffle bag in hand, Castro found Joel sipping on a glass of vodka while snuggled into a cream-colored couch, watching *Love and Hip Hop of Atlanta* on the oversized screen.

"Castro, is that you, hustler?" she stated in a flirtatious manner as she pulled out her nearly $20,000 smartphone by Vertu from her Louis Vuitton crocodile-leather bag.

"You already know," he responded in his black English as he walked into the posh entertainment room, his mind absorbing new ideas. "Let me borrow this for a second," he stated as he sank into the couch, grabbing the remote to change the channel, finding the local news station.

"I was watching that," she cried out, pressing her left hand over the mouthpiece of her phone.

"Shhh," he responded, pressing the volume button on the remote.

"It was said that around 2 p.m. today, two unknown masked men entered the establishment of 'Diamonds Are Forever' jewelry store with military weapons, forcing everyone to the floor," the newscaster continued. *"Witnesses stated that one of the undead mercenaries forced the owner*

to the back of the store, shooting and killing him before returning moments later to abduct the owner's wife. Dressed in Desert Storm fatigues, he demanded her to open the safe. There's no word on the condition of the woman at the present time. However, upon exiting the jewelry store, the robbers were confronted by two law enforcement officers responding to an automobile theft at a nearby clothing store. A fierce gun battle erupted and resulted in the death of both officers. Witnesses stated that one of the robbers was shot and wounded moments before the second man lifted him, and they escaped in a midnight-colored vehicle. There are no suspects at this time. If anyone has any information that could help apprehend or identify the two suspects responsible for such a terrible tragedy, you can call Durham Crime Stoppers at 919-WBA-Tipp. This is Catherine Singerton with WTVD 11 News . . . back to you, Larry."

"Fuck identifying who's ever responsible for the tragedy. I'd rather apprehend those diamonds they came off with," Joel stated into the phone as she stood and walked over to the minibar to pour herself another glass of wine.

"While you at it, fix me a glass," he instructed Joel, throwing a hundred-dollar bill her way. "Keep the change."

"Don't be bird feeding me, hustler," she stated as she reached down into the refrigerator to retrieve a bottle of Ace of Spades. "I like to wear five-thousand-dollar fur-embellished ankle boots."

"And I like to see you in 'em, that's why I do what I do," he stated while contemplating his next move.

"That's what hustlers do."

"No, Boo-Boo . . . hustling is not just something you do, it's who you are," she stated as she bent down to pick up the crisp one-hundred-dollar bill off the colorful fur carpet before taking a seat beside Castro. "What's in the duffle?"

"A couple hunnit thousand bands, and a gift for you," he stated as he reached into the duffle, removing a small silver box. "Tell whoever you talking to, you'll get at 'em later," he demanded.

"Don't play with me, Castro."

"Do I ever play with your emotions? I really do have a surprise for you," he stated as he withdrew the exquisitely crafted flawless diamond, which was set in a platinum band—an amazingly spectacular token to commemorate an alliance of seismic proportions.

"Oh my God, this is beautiful, Castro!" she stated, amazed at the beauty of its clarity. "Tyshineak, let me call you right back," she stated before pressing the end button.

"Joel, believe it or not, but falling in love with you has been amazing. I couldn't imagine anything better, until I found something even more official staying in love with you. Ma, you are truly a dope boy's dream who will always have my heart . . . will you marry me?" he stated as he slid the ring onto her engagement finger.

With radiant eyes, she eyed the 18-carat diamond before leaping into his arms, kissing him passionately before she abruptly paused and sprinted out of the entertainment room.

"Ma, where you going?" he stated, puzzled.

"Stay right here, don't move, daddy," she crooned softly.

Seconds later, she returned with a gift bag that read 'Diamonds Are Forever' and reached into the bag, pulling out a huge velvet box.

"This is for you, hustler," she slowly retrieved the box in silence, unaware of what to expect, and grasped the contents.

"What'cha got for me?" he asked, staring at the contents of the case.

"A gift I picked up for you—"

"Oh, hell yeah," he responded as he removed the diamond-clustered bracelet from its box. He'd longed to purchase one but neglected it because of the eighty-thousand-dollar price tag. "You got me looking so icy now!" he stated, eyeing the chunky bracelet wrapped around his wrist. "This your moment, ma, and I refuse to steal it!"

"Nooo, this is our moment," she said, grasping it as she adored her engagement ring.

"That's an understatement. I love it, daddy," she responded, pulling him into her arms.

Just as the husband and wife-to-be entered the master bedroom, his cell phone rang. "Talk to me," he answered.

"Bruh, I just caught one slipping, I need you to come through," Snatch stated, breathing rigorously.

"Where you at?"

"On Hollywood."

"I'm on my way . . . angel dust."

"Say it two times."

Castro quickly changed into a new set of clothing, strapped on his vest, grabbed his choice of weaponry as Joel questioned him while he trotted out the door. Once inside the garage, he jumped into one of his many toys, a supercharged armored diamond-black Range Rover. While coasting out, he noticed Joel standing on the balcony, mumbling words and rolling her eyes. Castro knew she would be unsettled by him leaving during such an occasion, but he knew it was honor before bitch love.

With swiftness, he skillfully handled the Range Rover through the hewn iron gates into the night traffic headed toward the Southside. Arriving in a matter of minutes, he spotted a bullet-ridden Porsche Cayenne surrounded by a team of officers searching through it. Slithering, he coasted through the bleakly lit street corner, as one of the many officers' scanning eyes made contact with those of the driver.

Suddenly, his phone rang. He placed his tool into his lap before answering the phone: "Bruh, where you at?"

"On Lodge," Snatch whispered.

"Meet me on Hollywood, and be careful, 'cause they everywhere," he informed him.

"I'm headed that way . . . bruh, hold on."

Turning onto Hollywood, Castro noticed a patrol car slowly heading in his direction on the opposite side of the street.

"Bruh, where you at?" Castro asked.

"You just passed me."

"Hold up, one coming down," he responded while eyeing his comrade on one knee through the rearview mirror at the edge of the woods. The moment the cop car turned left, heading toward Lodge St., Castro slammed the Rover into reverse and backed up, stopping. Snatch then sprinted from the woods, jumping into the Jeep.

"Bruh, what the fuck you done got yourself into now?" Castro asked as Snatch slouched down low into the leather cushion. Castro lit a blunt and set off onto the city streets of Durham, heading nowhere in particular.

"I was just breezing through the hood, and outta nowhere, da nigga YaYo just pulled up to the curb—"

"What da fuck he doing out here?" Castro asked, knowing YaYo had no business being in their Vietnam-like neighborhood.

"When I pulled up, he was handing the nigga Brooks some work, so I jumped out and stepped to 'em. He tried to get fly out the mouth, so I hit bruh on speed dial and bruh told me to pop his top."

"You Gucci though, right?" Castro asked, glancing down at Snatch as he rounded the corner, glad Snatch hadn't been arrested for murdering YaYo.

"Yeah, I'm good. That shit only added heat to my hotness," he snarled in his street lingo.

"So bruh gave the order?" Castro asked.

Snatch then explained that Malik felt as though YaYo may have had something to do with Ceelo's death and was now flooding the streets of Durham with the same product that was meant for ZooGang family.

"I don't believe Money move like that. Quiet as kept, I heard it was Face and them, but you know how the streets be promoting false gossip."

"I heard something similar. You know he just copped the new black-on-black Maserati. He came through the hood yesterday and threw like fifteen bands for the kids and kept it moving, like it was nothing," Snatch explained, recapturing the moment.

"Yeah, I seen 'em at the rim shop earlier, but dig this, our new jewelry connect copped all that shit. Here, I kept this one for you," Castro said, handing him a diamond-beaded necklace.

"You got me looking all flawless, shining and shit... good looking, bruh-bruh... dude copped all dem shits?"

"All of it," Castro said, making the right gesture. "But here's the plan. Since bruh already got the plug, I'ma drop a hunnit bands on 'em and let 'em know to holler at us when he touch."

"Do what it do, bruh. Whatever it's gone take to put us where we need to be... I'm wit' it."

As Castro coasted through the city, he and Snatch spoke of future endeavors, places they wanted to visit, and how much money they wanted to retire with after winning consecutive championships in the dope game. The night was still young, and the two hustlers had high spirits, so they decided to investigate further on the situation with YaYo. They were curious to know how long YaYo had been supplying work on their land and decided to visit a few rap spots. Before reaching their destination, they spotted a crackhead named Pookie walking down Hillside Street.

The duo exited the Range and began their fact-finding mission. Through Pookie's loose lips, they learned that YaYo had been handing out samples for the past month and that one of YaYo's baby mothers had come down from Winston-Salem and secured five trap houses in her name for his minions to move work out of. Realizing that YaYo was attempting to put himself in position to dominate the streets of Durham, Castro wondered if Jade and Carla supported his vision in any form. So he asked Pookie, knowing the crackhead knew just about anything that went on in the streets when drugs were involved. Pookie claimed he wasn't sure if Jade was involved, but word on the curb was that Carla was the one who introduced YaYo and his second-in-command to a couple of mid-level hustlers, and that she had been traveling back and forth to Houston, transporting massive amounts of dog food and an impressive amount of cash for YaYo. Castro and Snatch looked at one another, now realizing why Carla had been moving the way she had been moving, flying from city to city frequently.

"Bruh, let's go dead that bitch, now," Snatch whispered as they both climbed back into the Range Rover.

"Don't worry . . . her days are numbered. For every action, one must suffer the consequences," Castro stated, cutting in.

"You think we should enlighten Jade?"

"Nah, Jay already got a lot of other shit going on. Besides, she's a short fuse."

"More or less," Snatch agreed. Seconds later, his phone rang. Looking at the screen, he noticed it was Malik, so he answered.

"Red Rum Salute."

"Red Rum Salute . . . you wit' bruh?" Malik asked.

"You already know," Snatch said in his hustler lingo.

"You take that trash out?"

"Yeah, I took care of it ASAP," Snatch stated, indicating he had deaded YaYo.

"I got some'em for you, put bruh on the phone."

"Angel Dust."

"Red Rum Salute," Castro saluted.

"Everything a go on our end, we waiting on you."

"I'm laid up right now . . . just come through in the morning."

"Will do," Castro stated before ending the call.

Upon waking the following morning, Malik discovered that Destiny had snuck out once again undetected. Something she had mastered while dealing with each client. As he glanced upon his timepiece, noticing it was 9:30 a.m., which gave him an hour to shower, dress, eat, and smoke a blunt of purple before his confidants arrived to conduct and discuss business.

Less than twenty minutes later, feeling refreshed, he stepped out on the front porch into the early morning sun, just as Destiny pulled into the driveway in her silver CL600 Benz Coupe, a gift from Malik. He watched as she parked behind his Maserati, stepping out in seductive clothing all by U-Neak, revealing her perfectly shaped body in yellow stilettos, as her hair glistened in micro braids, resembling dreads. He looked on in silence, admiring her beauty, style, and swagger.

"Where the fuck you been?" he asked, as if it was the way a gangsta greeted his side chick early in the morning. However, he wasn't upset with her; it was just his awkward way of showing her he cared. She was aware of his incorrigible amorality; it didn't matter because she had long ago discovered his weakness. He couldn't control himself; he actually was a slave to sin and sex.

"I went to Hair Estate to get my hair done," she said while modeling for him. "You like?" she whispered in his ear as she walked past him, patting the bulge in his thousand-dollar jeans, smiling. He glanced down as she sauntered her way past him, looking at her voluptuous apple bottom, amused at how it shivered and rippled with each step she took.

However, she could feel his eyes forcing their way in between her thighs without being wanted.

"Are you undressing me with your eyes, Malik? If you want more of me, all you have to do is ask, but be prepared to suffer the consequences."

"Consequences are actually beneficial; it's the disloyal shit I dislike in you. You got me curious as to who you really are, the way you be moving. With me, it's not what you do that has me puzzled at times, but how you do it. Ma, I fuck with you to the max, but you move deceitfully at times, which has me feeling some type of way."

"Deceitfully . . . how can you fix your mouth to say some shit like that? If anything, you want to control me, which will never happen. I'm loyal to you, Malik, despite what you think of me," she said, spinning on her heels, entering the condo before he could vocalize his opinion, satisfied that she uttered the last word.

Hearing laughter behind him and a car door slam, Malik turned to face the three hustlers walking up the driveway towards him. "Damn," Castro barked, sounding like Kevin Hart. "Shawt got a cold body, big hips, and much bottoms. You sure you can handle all that ass, big homie?" he joked, as Snatch and Hysheem trailed closely behind with silly grins masking their faces.

"Oh word . . . that's how we do now?" Malik shot back as Castro stepped onto the top step. "Remember that when it comes back to you now. Oh, and congratulations on your engagement. I bet'cha didn't tell the homies that, now did you?" Castro dropped his head the moment he heard engagement, his sudden expression one of surprise. "Did I say something wrong? You the one made that decision, not me."

"Whatever," Castro shot back as his confidants exploded in laughter. "How the fuck you find out anyway?"

"It's obvious . . . a bitch gone always be a bitch... they run and tell this, and they run and tell that. That's why you gotta be extra mindful of what you say around 'em."

The laughter and joking continued as they sat on the balcony, smoking blunt after blunt with no seemingly adverse effects, while listening to Rick Ross that Destiny had blasting from within the condo. While getting incredibly stoned, all four generals discussed in detail how they would go about distributing the majority of their supply within the city limits and surrounding areas. Malik suggested they should step inside to discuss further business after noticing the same BMW circle the block three times. As Malik, Hysheem, and Snatch entered the condo, Castro ran back to his Jeep to grab the duffle, which contained a pile of capital totaling one hundred thousand. Destiny, who was on the phone, abruptly ended the call without warning or indication to whoever she had been talking to that she was ending the call, which was becoming normal for her.

"Who was you just on the phone talking to?" Malik asked, finding it strange how she quickly ended the call as he entered the living room.

"I was trying to reach my doctor, why?"

"Oh, you pregnant now?" Malik asked, suspicious of her actions.

"Boy, bye," she responded sharply. "Entertain your company and leave me alone."

"Let me find out," he paused. "Look… go grab that duffle bag for me."

Agreeing she would, Malik and his confidants seated themselves on the sofa just as Castro entered the condo, duffle in hand, placing it on the coffee table. Destiny rounded the corner seconds later, placing Malik's duffle alongside Malik's.

"If you need me, I'll be in the bedroom," she said softly. Once she exited, Malik noticed everyone eyeing the duffle bag in suspense.

He then opened it, exposing the contents inside.

"Bruh, you stay going hard for the team," Castro whispered, amazed at the individually wrapped kilos of heroin.

"You know I always take care of the offense in the fourth," Malik insisted. "We didn't team up, play together and make sacrifices to not want a championship. To be in the finals last year with Ceelo and lose, my desire is much stronger now. But there's steps we gotta take in order to get back to where we wanna be. But regardless, whether it be steps, levels or series, we will take them and win them," he stated while munching on a bag of jalapeño potato chips.

"So you already seen your peoples out Midwest," Castro mentioned between sips from a tequila bottle he brought from his Jeep.

"Nah, quiet as kept, Ceelo kept work at Destiny's spot, so she found dem shits and fronted 'em, but keep that internal . . . among us. Not even Jade should know this."

"So once we flood the streets with work and our profit improves, where the next shipment gone come from?" Snatch asked, while lighting a blunt.

"Midwest," Malik stated, lowering his voice so only those around him could hear. "Bruh, ain't I tell you I linked up with a solid mid-level distributor who can provide us with whatever we want for the low?" Malik continued as Snatch handed him a blunt the size of a small baguette.

Besides Malik, Hyseem was the only other hustler from the pool of individuals in the room who had the privileged knowledge of where the kilos actually came from. However, he sat in silence while Malik painted the perfect picture of the marching outline of the future.

"Well, here go a hunnit bands from me and Snatch to put in the pot," Castro stated, opening the duffle bag. "So, dude out Midwest . . . when do we meet him?" he retorted, dragging on the blunt, before passing it to Hysheem.

"Soon," Malik stated, not wanting to disclose too much information.

"You need a shield?'

"I would love for you to travel with me, but to play it safe, I've decided to travel alone to ease dude's mind-set, 'cause he on some paranoia shit right now," he stated, unsure if Castro would buy into his well thought out plan.

"Dude was kinda 'noid when he seen me in the car," Hysheem stated, playing his role in a fashion we must all play in order to advance the vision.

"Word, he was *noid*, bruh?" Castro stated, seeing the vision much clearer now.

"More or less . . . but don't worry, I got this. When the opportunity presents itself for us to march in and clean out the safe, you'll be the first to know," he stated in a braggadocious tone, while glancing briefly into Castro's duffle bag.

Hysheem smiled, observing Castro and Snatch as they absorbed the calculated language that was translated before them like foot soldiers, giving him and Malik confidence that their vision to diversity their revenue streams outline had clarified their vision, unfolding their route as they continued to move forward into the playoffs.

Although the two significant players of the dream team moved deceptively toward their teammates, their outline was masterminded to put them at a level of success they believed would satisfy and ensure everyone unlimited capital. To Malik and Hysheem, life was more like a combination lock; each day they would set out to find the right numbers in the right order so they could have everything they desired. In order to succeed, one must take risks. Everything you do must be an expression of your purpose. If an activity doesn't fit the formula, you shouldn't indulge in it—period. Because everything that happens to you is the result of your past actions and characteristics . . . therefore, some consequences are actually beneficial.

Chapter 5

"Nothing Ventured…Nothing gained"
-Malik-

During the following weeks, Malik and Hysheem shook the city by reinforcing maximum pressure throughout the city of Medicine, seeking the face of a 6'3", 290-lb dark-complexioned bushy-beard mid-level dealer. However, the gargantuan was nowhere to be found. No one had seen or heard from Zulu in months. The duo even visited Duke, where he had once attended school, seeking any information that could possibly lead to his whereabouts. But yet and still, their search led to a dead end, as all the students they had approached claimed Zulu had not attended any classes in nearly two semesters.

After their trial got colorless, they reasoned among themselves and concluded that Zulu had probably migrated and was living the extraordinary life he had created for himself in Miami. However, Malik kept his mission in motion and, before long, the entire pursuit team poured in. Anytime the team needed an assignment such as this one done, Malik would send either Jade or Rachel. Once in the presence of these instruments of power, their rivals became so obsessed that they let their kingdom fall to pieces, allowing Malik and Hysheem to march in and conquer without a fight.

Having come up ineffective baffled Malik, so Rachel questioned the physical sensation he was currently feeling.

A part of him seemed so infuriated because his search for Zulu hadn't unfolded as he anticipated, but yet and still, there was a side of him that seemed motivated to keep moving in the direction of his goal until he got there.

Weeks later, on a quiet night somewhere in a far more posh neighborhood north of Charlotte, North Carolina, at one of Malik's executive private estates that actually was a distribution center, Malik stood on the balcony doing what dope boys do—making moves on his Vertu smartphone, priced at $20,000—as he watched Hysheem exit his Jeep Cherokee with two duffel bags, one in his left hand and the other slung over his shoulder. Both hustlers had work to do and felt as if the work they had already put in was never enough. No matter how hard they hustled, they paid attention to the game, their competitors, the results they were currently producing, and the benefits that it brought them daily.

"Bruh, you 'bout ready to prepare this food?" Hysheem asked, referring to breaking the first ten kilos of heroin down into individual bundles.

"More-or-less . . . but we gotta keep the streets starving 'cause it got a mean appetite," he gushed. "Hold up, let me take a piss real quick," he stated, walking through the master-bedroom suite into his private bathroom.

Inside the bathroom, he reached into the custom cabinets and pulled out a box of latex gloves, tossing them on the counter. He then turned on the water and cupped his hands under the faucet, splashing cold water onto his face, looking into the mirror at his image and grasping his thoughts— staring into his face as if it was a second figure that resembled him, elbowing his way back into existence. The reflection aroused with an artful glance, holding the left side of his face in a snarl as if smoke from the flames of Hell had risen to consume his eyes.

"Red Rum Salute . . . what? You thought I was just gone fa' back and let you take all the credit for all the work I've put in?" his alter-ego, Young Money, said, muscling his way into the picture.

"Red Rum Salute," Malik stated, greeting Young Money. "Nah, bruh, you know it ain't like that. I'm just trying to take the position that I've always had—the power to make a difference in order to produce the desired result . . . it's that simple."

"What the fuck you mean, it's that simple? Nigga, if it wasn't for me, you wouldn't be where you at now, college boy," Young Money stated, sounding cocky. "Every five-star general has a powerful team of key members who do most of the grinding while he creates new resources and opportunities so the team can win multiple championships. You, of all people, should know there ain't no I in team—it's us against them—so play your position and let me play mine, 'cause like yourself, I got big dreams, and big dreams attract big people," he drilled. "Every team needs a big man."

"I ain't got no problem with you claiming your rep as the league's best big man," Malik stated, backing his words with fearless penetration, "but you know the point runs the floor."

"More-or-less . . . but at the same time, I got a vision for what I'd like to see come to pass—but I need you to realize I'm no longer coming off the bench no more as your sixth man. From now on . . . every action's gonna be done under my control. I'm the go-to guy who will push the team into the play-offs, and as I win, we win. Call me Kream now," Young Money asserted, transforming before Malik's eyes.

"If you gonna be the team's charismatic face who will make the team stronger and richer, then do what you do—by showing me through your actions. That's the difference between us and them. We do this shit. So let's put our egos aside and position ourselves so we all can win on every level . . . nothing ventured . . . nothing gained."

From that moment on, every action or decision made was under Kream's control. He transcended from basketball and became the ultimate dope boy—pushing everything from crack to heroin. Within a year, he reached the status he had spoken of and was no longer called Malik but Kream, for his uncanny ability to produce. Word throughout the streets spread quickly of the vacancy in the drug market since Ceelo's void—while striving to get to the top because the bottom was too overcrowded. However, Kream was able to undercut the competition because he had access to such a vast supply, surrounding himself with arrogant confidants who provided him with excellent information, helping him make loyal decisions. He also had shooters on deck who served as guardian angels—refusing to identify their sources in the face of dire threats and legal consequences. His angels were solid, brave underlings who pumped lifeblood of loyalty and wise counsel into his endeavors and ran errands before receiving high-level positions on his team, joining his incorporation . . . ZooGang. He taught his minions how to be a quick study and keep their mindset on whatever venture offered the most realistic opportunity to make the most money. Young Money's family was one of the most massive organizations in North Carolina. According to street accounts, the group nettled more than $5,000,000 a week peddling heroin from Durham to New Orleans. Exceptionally large sums of capital showed in everything they touched, along with the celebrities and hood models they encountered who tossed thongs at them as higher achievers. Kream created a legacy that inspired other hustlers—such as his accountability partner Hysheem Hunter—to dream more, learn more, do more, and become more.

"Bruh, any and everything you do must be conducted by a broad—but not just any broad. She gotta be the hottest commodity in the streets with a flawless face and impeccable taste, with a style of hustling that's dynamic and multifaceted but 100% real. She must know people—and I mean solid people," Kream stated . . . sharing one of his principles concerning ways to finance his capital throughout the local cities. "You just can't pull up to these small towns, post up and flood the hood with food. Meet a broad, observe her ways carefully a few days, then befriend her. In this field of work, life-planning and moving like a 'bawse' is how you score. Yet the real fun is not in simply scoring—rather . . . it's the excitement you get from coming up with creativity to reach the goal. But, in the process, you gotta spend time with her, and splurge on her until she recognizes you as the most thorough-lest dude in her life, and the excitement overwhelms her to the point she starts chit-chatting with her friends, spreading your name. Then once the streets discover the fact that you're a bawse, they'll want to do business with you in hopes you become their new supplier with food for the low-low. If all goes as planned... within weeks, an explosion of food will hit the streets, the blocks will be fed, and everybody will be eating from our table. The results will be miraculous—and you will be that dude that made it happen. Always remember, bruh, in order to excel you gotta become an asset for the streets, and the money will follow," he stated, sharing the wisdom he'd gathered from Jade, who was once his primary instructor.

Once the visualization activated the creative powers of Hysheem's subconscious mind, Kream armed him with killers and gang-bangers who hustled, ammunition, a quarter-million dollars, and numerous wrapped kilos to distribute throughout the smaller towns, while he, Castro, Snatch, and his guardian angels dominated the larger cities with force—gradually working their way into the finals.

"You know what, Hysheem?" the statuesque beauty known to all in Rocky Mount as Stacey, the numero uno of the hood, said. "I introduced you to shots—what? Like eight months ago—and now look. You damn near supplying the whole Murder Mount with food," she chirped happily, while lounging on the cream-colored couch painting her toenails.

She stood and walked toward the drawer where her U-Neak purse sat, reached into it and removed a wad of cash and placed it before him. Hysheem continued to sip from his expensive water bottle, staring at her, holding the bulge in his ZooGang jeans as she paraded around the condo in a skimpy skirt, which accented her super-thick Apple Bottom derriere. The sight of the 5-foot-3 straight-stunting model with golden brown skin, deadly slanted green eyes, thinly penciled eyebrows, and flame-red hair pulled back into a severe bun deserved a second look. "All my girlfriends know you get money, but they don't understand why you don't ball like one," Stacey said, a slippery-talker with a gift for open-end answers, leading herself into misinterpretations in ways that burnish her mythology.

"It's not my season to ball, and besides, why we wasting our time talking about them? That's what they do . . . we get money on a whole 'nother level they'll never reach. That's why they hate the fact you with me and not them. Tell them bitches only one thing matter to me, and that's accomplishing what I came out here to accomplish."

"I feel you, but this shit is like a game of Monopoly, Boo-Boo. In order for you to accomplish whatever it is you tryin' to accomplish, you gotta move like you move in suspense. But at some point, you gotta take them chances. You gotta floss at some point and push yourself beyond your limits."

"More or less . . . but you gotta know your limitations," he added, as he glanced down at his 112 Time designer, made by Chanel. "Don't get it twisted, shawty. I can floss at any level, at any cost—from summer to summer—but at *my* pace though. How many niggas you know in the hood can touch a mil right now?"

"I know you sittin' on a mil plus. I helped you count it, remember? But regardless of what you got or what you did to get it, I fuck with you to the max—no ulterior motive." Hysheem only smiled. Stacey had the most beautiful eyes he had ever seen.

Remaining silent, Stacey began massaging the back of his neck affectionately—the ultimate seduction to lift his thoughts into the clouds in hopes to relax him before moving in to conquer her mission.

"Hysheem, remember the night we met at Trina's birthday bash at Club Dream in Miami?" she asked, changing the subject to prevent from ruining her spell. "You were stunting in ya lil Maserati Coupé."

"That's what we do when we hit the stage—parking-lot pimping, baby."

"Boy, bye."

"Shawty, I can't lie, but you stole my heart that night—lookin' like a real Egyptian doll with a million-dollar mindset . . . your whole clique deserved a second look, but you had my undivided attention." He nuzzled the back of her neck, kissed her, and fondled her famous booty.

"Then you took me to that strip club and we ran into your entourage," she continued as her fingertips caressed his chest. "It was so many of them—gold bottles galore . . . and that one guy," she laughed, replaying the event in her mind. "He had everybody crackin' the fuck up."

"Who, Roc-Boy?" he remembered. "He's a storyteller," he stated, as he stripped off his *No New Friends* tee shirt, exposing the tattoos that covered 80 percent of his slim frame.

Checking himself in the mirror, Stacey took a moment to admire his handsomeness, with approval gleaming in her eyes. She adored his dope-boy swag—even though he wasn't expensively clad in Gucci, he was impressing in a New Era fitted over tightly bound dreads with a crisp pair of jeans, preferably by ZooGang.

Suddenly, with intensely heartfelt emotions, Stacey whispered, "I love you, Hysheem."

"I love you more," he responded, looking over his shoulder. "What's so funny?" he thundered, walking toward the hallway bathroom.

"You. You walk funny—but it's cute though."

"That's 'cause I'm hung, shawty. And if you keep clownin' me 'bout the way I walk, your friends gon' be wonderin' why *you* walkin' the way *you* walkin' after I knock the bottom out that pussy tonight."

"Excuse me . . . who said you was gettin' some tonight?" she teased. "This kitten is on lockdown. If anything, all you may get is some head," she giggled.

After draining himself in the toilet, he washed his hands, opened the cabinet, and removed a container filled with Vaseline. He then exited the bathroom, headed in the direction of the living room with a smirk on his face. Entering the now semi-darkness of the living room, he called out for Stacey, who responded from the bathroom.

As he entered the room, Beyoncé played softly on the compact sound system. An arousal formed between his legs as he thought back to the night his dick slid in between Cubana Lust's thighs—a twenty-five-year-old internet vixen he'd met at Hot 107.9's birthday bash in Atlanta one night, and experienced anal sex.

Startled at the sight, all thoughts of Cubana Lust were quickly tossed aside as he stared at Stacey in astonishment. Standing at the threshold of the king-size bed, Hysheem held a hungry stare.

Stacey stood completely nude, with his diamond-beaded ZooGang necklace descending between her cleavage, as her breasts jutted out firmly—their soft, swollen tips erect as moisture dottled the exquisite pubic triangle between her thighs. Neither one took their eyes off the other. Stacey enjoyed the delight and appreciation she saw each time in his eyes at the sight of her perfection.

"You're a goddess," he said, unable to take his eyes off her.

"And you're one of the sexiest men in the streets," she said, looking at his chest. It was broad and muscular. "What's that for?" she asked, pointing at the Vaseline container in his hand.

"For us," he said, placing the container on the dresser. "I want to explore you tonight."

"Explore me . . . .?" she asked with an artful glance. "In what way?"

"Anally."

"Boy, bye," you ain't 'bout to stick that thick dick in my ass."

"Shawty, stop crying . . . shit! Who knows, it might bring us closer, if it's done right. Just act like you shitting in reverse," he laughed, jokingly.

"I don't see shit funny," she replied, climbing onto the bed.

"Why are you so afraid of anal sex?" he asked, as he sat on the edge of the bed to tug off his boots, but never took his expectant eyes off of her.

"It's not that I'm afraid. Actually, I love the way it feels when you be holding my waist and pushing my back down while you be fucking the shit out of me, but I was told that anal shit hurts . . . besides, your shit supra-thick, daddy."

"Ma, I promise be easy. If you don't like it I'll pull out."

"You promise to be gentle?'

"I promise . . . you'll 'bout to experience a sensational feeling like no other."

"Don't hurt me, daddy," she stated softly as she stroked the front of his *True Religion* jeans. Finding his zipper, she pulled it down carefully over his bulge. She then reached inside and her fingers fumbled with his boxers for a few seconds before she was able to free his solid and thick erection from its denim jeans. He stroked her hair and she looked up like a supplicant maiden about to steal his power.

Her tongue protruded from between her moist lips, and its tip touched the head of his penis, which jerked like a heartbeat in her warm hands. She smiled to herself, then pulled him toward her so that she could take him in her mouth. Hysheem was massive in size and thick, but she was able to slide his dick into her throat and be fully in possession of him.

She moved her head up and down until she sensed the danger that he might explode too soon from the pleasure of his member moving in and out of her wet mouth. She pulled away reluctantly and pressed her face into his muscular thigh.

"Hold up," he mumbled, as he motioned for her to pause for a moment. He stood up, then walked awkwardly across the room and stumbled onto a shoe made by Christian Louboutin, priced at $895.00, before finding the light switch and switching it on. Light spilled over the room onto them, and Stacey blinked as if awakening from a dream.

"Let's fuck wit' the lights on," he stated, because he knew this would be the last time he would connect flesh-to-flesh with her before he left Rock City for good.

He stretched out on her Versace sheets. His big hands covered her breasts as she half-closed her eyes, expecting that next she would feel his weight on her and then feel his thick member sliding between her thighs. She was ready for him—already moving her hips restlessly—but he surprised her by slipping down her body and pushing her thighs apart. He clasped her derriere in his hands again, and her moist vagina opened to him like a ripe red fruit. She expected that he would plunge his face into her, but once again he surprised her by slipping two fingers into her tight slit and touching her in a spot that was going to flood his fingers with her juices.

"Ohhh," she groaned, squeezing her eyes shut and thrashing her sex kitten against his hand. "Hysheem, what are you doing to me? I'm going to burst if you don't stop that."

But he wouldn't stop. The frenzy mounted in her. Her first orgasm was like a faucet he'd turned on and she couldn't turn off. The second left her gasping. She didn't think she could take a third.

He was incredibly sensitive to her, as if he knew that she couldn't take any more. He withdrew his fingers and replaced them with his tongue. He moved it so slowly and in such tiny, fluttery motions that it soothed her overexcited nerve endings. He seemed to empathize so closely with her reactions that she was blown away. How could he know so much about what turned her on? Surely, only another woman could possibly know how to play your body like a stringed instrument.

"You taste so good that I could stay in this position all night," he told her.

"Take control of me," she replied. "Put it in my ass and give me all you got."

Hysheem reached for the container of Vaseline, removed the lid, and slowly massaged the Vaseline onto his member, then entered her with the calmly assured ease of a man entering his own house. Balanced above him on knees and elbows, he slid easily and lightly into her anal, and then held her just as lightly in his arms when he began to move. He felt bigger inside her than she'd expected. She could feel the tip of his penis knocking at the door of her womb. Although he held her in his arms, his heavy, muscular body still didn't touch her, as she fantasized that she was making a movie. She was Kim Kardashian, and he was Ray J.

But just as she was getting used to his slow, gently probing—just as she was adjusting to the exquisite sensation of his penis inside her anal, throbbing and moving almost imperceptibly back and forth—he changed his rhythm and began to move faster, as if he had judged that she was open and deep enough now to contain the force of full desire.

Lust swelled in them as they crashed against each other with such energy they threatened to gallop off the bed. Their rhythms of thrust and reception, push and pull—were those of rowers moving against the current, moving to catch up with the trajectory of their desire.

When it happened like this, it was so fantastic that Stacey held nothing back. She heard a strange, hoarse sound in the room and opened her eyes to look for the source, but it was coming from her—low moaning, almost like the growling of an animal. She was so full of him in those minutes of stark intimacy—so filled. Not merely with his flesh, but with his very being, his erotic essence—that she could forget herself and surrender to him the way a surfer surrenders to a wave.

"Oh, Hysheem," she babbled helplessly. "Don't stop, please don't stop."

His firm lips covered hers. His tongue darted in and out of her mouth. Then he delivered a long, deep kiss that assured her he wouldn't stop, not now . . . Impossible as it seemed, he moved faster, as if redoubling his efforts to drive himself into her—to fuse their beings in eros. She could no longer keep up with him; her energy flagged at last, and all that she could do was hold on while the storm raged above her and into her.

She closed her eyes, and when she did, he lowered his body until she felt all of his weight on her at last. The closeness of it was incredibly sensuous. He wasn't heavy, but he covered her everywhere, and a live electric current arced between the tip of his tongue down through her body to the top of his member.

Suddenly, he stopped moving. She opened her eyes and watched his face. He ground his teeth together, fluttered his eyelashes, and began to tremble from head to toe. She felt his climax first as an electrical charge zapping her secret opening—then he went rigid from head to toe for one incredible, heart-stopping moment. Then the dam broke, and his hot seed spilled inside her.

She pulled him into her, moved her hips to meet his last crashing thrusts, and savored the last feeble jets of semen that spurted from him. Her encouragement made him even more frantic to unite with her, which brought on an overwhelming orgasm that left her gasping and speechless.

When the storm was over and they were still at last, it seemed natural when he wrapped his arms around her and pulled her to his tatted chest. She could hear the pounding of his heart. She wondered dreamily—still lost in the twilight zone between sex and the return to sanity—why it had been so good, but she wasn't able to analyze the chemistry of it. She almost always had a good time in bed, but very few of her lovers had brought her to this state of rapturous animal contentment.

Chapter 6

"I came, I saw, I conquered"
-Hysheem-

On a cool Monday evening in May, Hysheem pulled up in front of Shot's grandmother's house in his highly desired diamond-black Aston Martin. Stepping out of the driver's side door, clad in Christian Louboutin sneakers and a custom-made leather baseball jersey, the letters stretching across his chest announced his arrival—an essential aspect of his identity—and a message he brought to the streets . . . ZooGang.

"So you out for good, fam?" the caramel-complexioned, five-eight, young *Future* look-a-like questioned.

"You already know . . . but the grind doesn't stop. I won't let it!" he stated, surveying his surroundings from behind a pair of eight-thousand-dollar pitch-black shades.

"My time has expired out here. I came, I saw, I conquered; it's on you now to keep the hood fed. Everything starts wit' a leader, and from what I've seen, bruh, you're extremely influential in the hood. So strive to live intentionally and remember that whatever setting you find yourself in, a lot of eyes gon' be on you—seeing shit you won't even realize you modeling."

"More or less," Shots stated, reaching into his Prada windbreaker and pulling a cigarette from one of his pockets. "I do what I do for my hood. That's why I be going so hard. I wanna win, and I'm willing to do whatever it gon' take to make that happen."

"It's already happening," Hysheem stated, thumbing a button on a little black box attached to his key, lowering the passenger-side window to his V12 Virage Coupe as Future's melodious, auto-tune-tinged dope boy soliloquies simultaneously thundered to life through the canyons. "But it's a competitive game, and you have to constantly be like, what's my next move?"

"But you came out here and played the game like a wizard—"

"But everything I did was thought through. When I came out here, I had a plan. I snatched a broad, and she introduced me to the top hustler. Now he playin' team ball, and we winnin'."

Shots could be trusted, but he was to be fed information in small doses.

The two continued to converse and caught up on the word on the curb—who and who not to draft, where the newest heroin source was, who was being shadowed by the feds— the usual idle chit-chat of small-time crooks still dreaming of riches.

"I'm trying to be like you, Hy—reclined in leather seats. How do I get that level of success?" he stated, lighting his second cigarette.

"Shit takes time," Hysheem said, thorough and unruffled. "You can't sprint through this shit."

"So once I'm done wit' what I got, you got more for me?"

"Get what you already got done, and we'll discuss next week what's next for you."

"Fo' sho."

"Look, I'm 'bout to bounce," Hysheem stated, as he opened the driver's side door and slid behind the wheel. "I gotta take care of a few more things before I head South. So you be safe."

His phone rang. He answered it. "Hold on, bruh-bruh."

"The opportunity has presented itself for you to represent your hood. So do what you gotta do and make history, fam."

"I'm on it . . . Angel Dust."

"Say it two times," Hysheem stated, as he cranked the engine by pushing a button and sped away. "Red Rum Salute," he barked into the phone.

"I take it our work is done out there?"

Kream said, "How's Stacey taking it?"

"Oh, she good." He paused to think. "She just hated to see me go . . . but she respects my vision though."

"Nah, I just can't stop fuckin' with shawty like that. She knows the game too well and understands her role as my companion."

"Your companion—"

"No doubt. Any dope boy with sense wants a chick who is domestic and got something going for herself."

"Bruh, I understand that, but you're overly obsessed with shawty's presence," Kream stated confidently.

Hysheem knew that Kream had stated a fact about him being obsessed with Stacey's presence, manner, and nonchalant air. Unexpectedly, Hysheem had fallen deeply in love with her, but he knew if he didn't unshackle himself from her compelling gaze, he might have lost focus and allowed his kingdom to fall to pieces, allowing those crooks to march in and conquer without a fight.

"Is this what this phone call is about?" Hysheem stated, as he handled the Aston Martin skillfully down Highway 64.

"Oh, you gettin' emotional?" he continued in a comical tune. "You know the motto—"

"Bruh, you gotta know how to capitalize on everything you do," Kream's voice crooned through the phone.

Suddenly erupting into a coughing fit, Hysheem removed the blunt from his mouth and composed himself while eyeballing the speedometer. He was doing 105 in a 65, easily.

"Bruh, how you know I was catchin' feelings?" Hysheem asked in shock.

There was a moment of silence in his ear.

"That's internal," Kream stated before the phone went dead.

Chapter 7

"End of Debate"
-Kream-

Arriving at the secluded stash house, Hysheem carefully pulled into the garage, closing the door behind him by remote. Exiting the vehicle, he stretched his arms while removing the money-filled duffle bag from the back seat. Flicking the lights on, he unlocked the door to the house, then quickly disarmed the security by pressing a code into the alarm panel.

The moment he stepped onto the marble floors, he moved cautiously, scanning the place visually in all directions. Entering the master bedroom suite, he sat on the edge of the bed, taking a moment to rid any memory of Stacey lingering in his mind just a day afterwards. Suddenly, willing such luminous memories to fade, he grabbed the remote to the built-in 125-inch screen plasma and flicked through the channels until finding BET. The moment the surround system thundered with music by Young Jeezy, he readjusted the volume and tossed the remote onto the king-sized bed.

Retrieving the duffle bag, he walked across the master suite into a room which appeared to be an oversized walk-in closet. With a touch of a hidden button, a portion of the back wall slid backward, allowing access to another walk-in closet that contained a biometric fingerprint-scanning safe.

Dropping the duffle to the floor, he entered a code, waited a second, then placed his fingerprints on the scanner.

Seconds later, a green light flashed and its steel door opened. Inside sat several rows of kilos and a total of 25.7 million dollars. It was every dope boy's dream to have such a large amount of cash, and he couldn't believe that he was standing in the midst of neatly stacked dead white guys meticulously wrapped in plastic. He whistled to himself, finding it hard to believe that such a dream had come to pass—and that an additional three million would be added once Snatch and Castro arrived from V.A., where it would then be counted and divided.

Falling to his knees, Hysheem tried making sense of the fact that Kream didn't sound like his coachable self over the phone. He sounded as if something heavy weighed on his mind. Hysheem knew well and thought in silence as he stacked the money from the duffle into the safe, knowing that Kream would discuss whatever problem he struggled with while hustling out in Chicago. Closing the safe, he stood to his feet when he heard shuffling footsteps moving about throughout the hallway, drawing closer to him.

Expeditiously, he snatched his .50 caliber from its hideaway holster and barked, "Kream, is that you?"—as if he was sending a complete and final warning while thumbing the hammer back.

"Who the fuck else is it supposed to be?" the voice quickly barked, knowing what was liable to transpire if he didn't respond back. "Don't nobody know about this spot but me and you, bruh, so let's keep it that way," he said, entering the master suite with a large duffle slung over one shoulder.

"Shit, you never know who's extorting who these days for they treasure. Niggas doing whatever it takes to get to our level. I trust no one outside my circle—that includes the feds."

"So you'll bust them hammers at 'em?" Kream challenged.

"If need be . . . shit, I refuse to let anybody slide up under me and my co-d and extort us for our treasures."

Kream smiled at his second-in-command's well-spoken words of loyalty. "Fuck whoever in the extortion business outside of us . . . we the motherfucking muscle. All we fear is them discovery and indictment papers."

"That's why I stay low key under the radar, fam."

"More or less . . . so what's been good, bruh-bruh?"

"I just been grinding, bruh-bruh, trying to get from where I am to where I wan' to be," stated the franchise player.

After neatly stacking all the proceeds from both duffles in the safe, both hustlers headed to the living room to blow on some exotic while playing *NBA 2K12* on the Xbox 360. The game was intense and extremely competitive between both competitors as though they were arch rivals. They played for numerous hours until thumbs and fingers pained from continuous action of pressing buttons.

"End of debate," Kream shouted after hitting the game-winning shot at the buzzer. "We now understand why LeBron is the best of all time."

"You can't be serious," Hysheem chuckled. "Magic was the most fearless penetration guard to ever play the game."

Both hustlers shared a few moments of laughter amongst one another while smoking on the highest grade of marijuana when suddenly Kream sunk into an enormous Carolina-blue bean bag beside Hysheem, a consequential impression masking his face.

"You know ole boy back in town, right?" Kream stated calmly, eyeing his accountability partner.

"Who?" Hysheem asked, while lighting a third blunt.

"Zulu—and he asking questions."

"Well, let's put our minds together and elevate what needs to be done . . . and move toward putting what we decide in motion."

Both hustlers figured that Zulu had left the city for good and held no clue that he would return to search out Ceelo's killers. However, what puzzled them even more was the fact that they were both in the blind because neither of them had any current information on Zulu—nor which shooters he had hired to put in work such as assassinations. To keep from facing the consequences of their previous actions, they needed to touch base with the streets in order to gather any and all solid information about their rival . . . their very life depended on it.

"It's a good thing we withdrew when we did and moved in the direction of feeding other cities and small towns, 'cause if we would have continued to be seen in the city, the more the streets would have talked."

"True story, but it seems as though our withdrawal made us more talked about—and even more admired. Now we gotta move aggressive and put maximum pressure on our competitors' defense."

"So what's the plan?" Hysheem asked.

"To get aggressive, and approach the situation with purpose—'cause dude didn't show back up to talk," Kream stated in his coachable tone. "I'm going on vacation with Jade in a few days, but while I'm gone, I need you to keep your eyes and ears open to the streets in case that fat bitch decides to show face."

"If I see 'em," Kream interjected, more than sure Hysheem would assassinate his intended target on sight. "It may open a door. If dude just lost a hunnit thou and still servin' the South wit food, then he's worth pursuing," he stated, just as his cell phone vibrated in his lap. "Talk to me."

Briefly, Kream spoke into the receiver of the phone before ending the call.

"Look, I gotta march out right quick. If nothing happens, I'll see you and the others at the studio in forty-eight."

"We still hosting Tyshineak's birthday bash."

"March 12th, right? We in the building," Young Money answered.

"It's not only her birthday bash, she's launching her new U-Neak heels," he paused.

"You crashing here tonight?"

"Nah, Kimbella hosting an event tonight in Charlotte, so I'ma meet her out there."

"Well, hit me in the A.M. . . . Angel Dust."

"Say it two times."

It was just a few moments before night when both hustlers jumped into their vehicles. Kream left in one car headed east of Raleigh, where he would spend the night with Rachel and then catch a flight to Cali the next morning to visit Bam, who was currently doing a federal bid on the West Coast. Hysheem went south as he blended into the midnight traffic en route to Charlotte . . . a city that knew him well.

Chapter 8

"He who deals with anyone is loyal to no one"
-Jade-

Like clockwork, forty-eight hours later, somewhere around 6:15 p.m., Kream, Hysheem, Castro, and Snatch sat around a large-sized table wrapping, counting, and packing money lavishly as they puffed on Raspberry blunts. Directly in front of each hustler sat a machine that conducted something different than the other, making their job much easier for them.

"Ten thousand!" Kream yelled over the money machine that counted with blurring speed. He then slid the stack of dead white guys to the right of him.

"Ten thousand!" Castro yelled seconds later. "Now being sealed," he added as he placed two-inch-thick stacks of money into the second machine that wrapped and sealed each stack in plastic.

Several heartbeats later, after Castro had wrapped the money, Snatch yelled, "Ten bands!" stamping its amount on top of the plastic and sliding it to the right of him.

"Ten band it is," Hysheem stated before placing the stack of bills into an armored duffel to be transferred to another location.

With discipline as if indoctrinated by a bank teller, all four hustlers had just completed a long and lengthy process counting millions of dollars. They were exhausted but knew the night had just gotten started, and they had more to accomplish still as a movement—despite the fact that their fingers were stiffening.

"Bruh-bruh, we still getting our Red Rum on tonight?" Hysheem questioned, sliding the last of the ten duffels across the floor.

Kream despised the fact that when he made mention of his next move to his circle of confidants, one of them turned around and second-guessed him. Warning his generals about such matters seemed to do no good, he thought to himself. However, he decided not to lose his composure.

"Bruh, when have you ever heard me say something and not mean it?" he answered calmly. "Ain't no outsiders gon' come within my limits and not pay taxes, and think they gon' dictate to my workers when, where, and how they can get money. Do these niggas know I run the city?" He paused to look each hustler in the eye with direct contact. "Y'all niggas looking at me like I ain't talking 'bout nothing. Y'all wit' me or what?"

"Fam, it's ZooGang till I die," Hysheem cut in. "I was just trying to see where yo mind was at, 'cause I know we got other shit in motion. But it's whatever. I'm always ready to let my hammer talk. I ain't shot nobody in a week."

"It's been three days for me," Snatch cut in.

"Y'all niggas crazy," Castro retorted. "But not as crazy as me." Brandishing a .357 Magnum from his waistline, he animated.

"Fuck all the talking, where these niggas at?" Snatch asked suddenly.

Everyone suddenly looked at each other with question marks in their eyes. They all knew that YaYa's comrades were in the Triangle trying to bully their way into the streets by taking control of two of Kream's trap spots in Raleigh.

"I'll never send y'all niggas out on a mission to danger which I will not myself encounter," he softly spoke while punching a series of numbers, as his confidants looked on in silence. "Baby girl, is everything in motion?" he asked, speaking into the phone. "That's what it do . . . I'll see you in thirty," he stated before ending the call.

"Bruh, who was that—Jade?" Castro questioned, sure Kream had just spoken to one of his 'Angels' in relation to what puzzled him.

"You'll learn more as the story unfolds," he advised calmly, with a wolfish grin masking his face. "Snatch, ride with Castro. It's time we take back what's rightfully ours, then head to Miami to make history."

Expeditiously, they stored all machines, dumped all the ashtrays, cleaned the house, and gathered all their personal effects such as guns, bulletproof vests, and the money they had split and divided equally. Briefly, they paused by two Honda Accords to discuss the events of the night and how they would approach each mission accordingly.

While tending to his drug operation and other business ventures, Kream had two of his guardian angels from Bragg Street keep a close eye on one of his rival competitors, who had been organizing, trying to engage in a takeover in one of his trap spots. Continuously, he had been updated with information concerning their movement—where they shopped, slept, and dined at. Even their companions' government names, along with current addresses—for when the war really jumped off.

After advising his confidants that he wanted them to be sober-minded, alert, and focused, he looked them all in their eyes to confirm they all understood—and the fact that each assassin had stood over fleshly murdered corpses and had lived through darkness of gun flashes that they had all agreed upon never to discuss with no one. During trapping season, shortly after the execution of Ceelo, members of ZooGang had bodied hustlers in Chicago, Tennessee, Memphis, Alabama, Atlanta, Maryland, New York, Virginia, and the Carolinas with sophisticated weaponry—as if they were kamikaze capitalists.

Moments later, after climbing into the two stolen Audis, they pulled out of the driveway with Kream leading as Castro and Snatch followed at a respective distance. Young Money checked his rearview mirror as he rounded a corner, making a left onto Bragg St. Passing his cell to Hysheem, he informed him to dial a number. Once the call had been placed, he took the phone back just as the receiving party answered.

"Ma, where you at?" he asked quickly. "I'm in the hood now . . . a'ight, I'll find it," he said before ending the call and pulling alongside an apartment building, killing the headlights. "Bruh, we looking for a CLK," he said, informing Hysheem. "There it go right there beside that gold Honda," he whispered. "Watch closely," he stated, glancing in the rearview mirror, noticing Castro had killed his lights as well, slowing his car to a crawl.

"What I'm looking for?" Hysheem asked wildly, peering out of the window in search of a silver Benz. "I don't see shit," he said in frustration when unexpectedly a car door being shut sounded through the quietness of the dark, catching his attention.

A southern-thick, angelic hood diva with long blonde hair appeared, strolling across the parking lot clutching an $8,000 Damier print bag made by Louis Vuitton, disappearing into a nearby apartment. Hysheem then shifted his gaze as Kream pulled behind a parked SUV. Moments later, a flash erupted in a car only a short distance away on the opposite side of the street.

"Smart move," Hysheem whispered, just as a curvaceous hood diva slithered out of the passenger side of the vehicle, closing her door behind her with calmness.

The hustler who had slid from the passenger-side door of the CLK gradually strolled down the sidewalk. She attempted to stay low behind her signature U-Neak shades. Hysheem tried to view the hustler's face but was unable due to the darkness. As she neared the vehicle, he gasped in disbelief upon recognizing the identity of the hottest commodity in the Carolinas.

"Red Rum salute!" Jade stated, greeting both killers as she discreetly folded herself in the seat directly behind Young Money. "Perfect timing, coach," she mumbled in a whisper that only he could hear, while removing ladylike Louis Vuitton gloves from her hands like what ZooGang presented to the streets was normal.

"He have loafers of bread like these streets say he did?" Kream asked, respecting a loyal answer.

Before speaking, Jade maintained silence for a second as Kream pulled away from the curb slowly.

"Yeah, he sitting on half a mil easily. He was so obsessed over me though."

"I expected him to be. Any real dude in the streets getting real money will at some point slip and allow his kingdom to fall to pieces when in your presence because of your seductiveness."

There was a silence.

"So what do I owe you?"

"My pink Bentley and a trip to Paris."

"I heard about the explosive work you and Rachel pulled off in Vegas. We definitely needed that one, 'cause none of us could've gotten that close to 'em without making a scene."

"I'll just play my position . . . it's ZooGang all day, Kream," she assured him.

"What's up with Miami?"

"It's still in motion," he paused. "But there's another situation we 'bout to approach before heading south . . . You in the mood to put in mo' work?" he asked, tossing her an extra mask. "We could use one more body."

Jade thought about his question for a moment and decided why not, being that she would be leaving the country soon with him on vacation.

"The circle wouldn't be complete without me . . . what do you have in mind?" she politely asked.

"Murder."

"Oh, I'm definitely with getting my Red Rum on . . . Who's hosting the event?"

"Dem Coke Boys."

"How many loafs involved?"

"I'm not sure. That's not my focus, but whatever we find, we take."

"I'm saying," Hysheem suddenly interjected, shifting in his seat and looking over his shoulder at Jade, "Did you ever find out where dude stash spot is?"

Feeling as if he had just asked a dumb question, she stared Hysheem down with a look of evilness.

"What?" he asked, shrugging his shoulder, recognizing her ill gaze.

"I found out everything we need to know."

"Even the combination?" Young Money asked while pulling up to a red light.

"What's wit' all these dumb-ass questions tonight?" she snapped back.

There was a burst of laughter as Kream's voice filled the car. Once the laughter ceased, he spoke thuggishly real.

"A'ight, we 'bout to circle back and snatch that. Then we pay these lames a visit," he advised.

"Nah, let's address these lames first, then reap the benefits," Jade suggested.

Agreeing with her, Kream coasted around corners, hit backstreets, and creeped his way towards Tristina Woods in Cary, as Jade and Hysheem loaded and readied their ammunition. He then pulled over on a side street and gave Hysheem the wheel so that he could fully ready himself for the assignment at hand.

"Fam, tighten up—we almost there," Hysheem informed the two while gun-checking themselves.

"I'm good," Kream spoke. "You ready, Ma?" he asked Jade.

"I just need a couple more seconds," she stated with an empty gun in hand. "Let me see that clip!" she asked with a Black Widow's voice.

Grabbing the clip to the chrome .40 cal Jade held in her hand, he gently passed it to her. Without uttering a word, she took it, slammed it home with an open palm, and pulled the slide back.

"*Wa-chink!*" the gun sounded as the slide slid forward, slamming a slug home in the bench.

"Damn!" Kream gasped. "You serious wit' it, ain't 'cha?" She stared into his eyes a second before looking away.

"It's like putting on heels . . . it's really nothing. I told 'cha I caught my first case at thirteen," she reminded him while checking the fit of her gloves.

Within a matter of seconds, they rounded the corner of Tristian Woods. Instantly spotting his contact's vehicle, Kream ordered Hysheem to pull over and park. He climbed out from the car.

"Be right back," he told his confidants as he walked off.

Both confidants sat in silence as they watched Kream, who was clad in all-black military-style cargo pants and its matching jacket.

"I see he got everything planned out perfectly," Jade informed Hysheem. "I feel sorry for whoever he's talking to, 'cause once the mission is accomplished, he gone off them too," she said, watching Kream as he stepped onto the sidewalk, using darkness to conceal himself as much as possible.

"A'ight, our target third floor, third door on the left," he informed all four killers as they exited the stolen vehicles brandishing big guns. "Let's serve justice."

Slowly, Kream climbed the stairs of the apartments, holding an all-blackened, subdued powder-coated finished M-16 that was glare-free in darkness. It held a thirty-round clip. Directly behind him, he was followed by Castro, who held a carbine fully automatic Uzi that was manufactured by the Russians. To his left, Snatch tight-gripped an AK-47, with Jade and Hysheem bringing up the rear. Meek Mill's newest mixtape blared from within the apartment, concealing their whispering from the ears of those inside.

"Hillary!" Kream whispered, turning his focus to Jade, who was wearing a mask that resembled Hillary Clinton. "You come in fast, directly behind Bill," he informed her.

Quietly, she nodded her head in agreement, just as Castro eased to the left side of the door with his Uzi on ugly. He peered over to his right, locking eyes with Kream's behind a Barack Obama mask. Kream then looked to Hysheem and Snatch, who both held their AKs aimed on the door. Gently, he nodded.

"*Blaaww!*" the door thundered a nanosecond after Snatch violently kicked it in with his 10½ boot. Without a moment to spare, all five killers rushed into the apartment, wildly peering around with careful eyes.

Spotting a jump-off on all fours, down between a gang member's legs giving him head—"Stay the fuck where you at, bitch!" Castro yelled, just as the chick jumped, startled by the crashing of the door.

"Get da fuck—" one of Kream's underlings, clad in a pair of sea-blue jeans exposing his tatted chest, yelled while desperately reaching for his ratchet on the table.

Blattt! Castro let off a sudden burst of lead, smashing holes into the worker's chest. The youngster grunted in pain, clutching his chest as his soul slowly slipped out of him. Suddenly, the room erupted in a crazed sound of thunderous explosions. A third underling appeared from thin air, busting a large cannon in his hand.

Jade instinctively dropped to the floor, taking cover behind a La-Z-Boy. Bullets splattered sheetrock from the wall slightly to her left and above the wall. Glancing towards the kitchen, aiming his ratchet at its intended target, she then aimed her chrome .40 cal and fired at the target—just as four more guns trained on him let off a sound of murderous shots. The figure then fell to the floor, after a hail of slugs riddled his body with large-sized holes.

Suddenly, there was a scream. A hood diva, who appeared to resemble Carla—Jade's best friend—desperately tried dashing for the door.

Springing into action, Jade swiftly moved into the path of the seductive diva, pointing her ratchet in the diva's face.

"Don't even think about it, bitch," she told her friend of fifteen years with a slight hint of shock masking her face, which Carla couldn't make out.

Jade was lost for words as Carla froze, pleading, "Hillary, I can explain . . . Pleeeaaasssee don't kill me."

Snatch, Castro, Hysheem, and Kream hastily hustled about the room and positioned themselves with an advantage on all points of the living room. The underling on the sofa, with his leather jeans still down around his ankles, demanded to know what was going on.

"Do it look like we came to talk?" Hysheem barked, before smacking him with his gun. "Break bread or Wake Med," he demanded, just as Jade pushed Carla onto the couch beside a second chick.

"Fuck you . . . I ain't breaking bread wit' shit. Get it how you live, nigga," the underling stated with boldness.

"Really!" Jade yelled, smacking the Gucci Mane look-a-like across the face with her gun. "Last warning. Give us what we came for, or else," she informed him.

"Or else what, bitch? Do what you came to do. I ain't coming off shit. It is what it is . . . straight like dat," he spit, unafraid to suffer the consequences.

Before anyone could utter another word, Jade aimed her gun at the naked diva who sat beside the Gucci Mane look-a-like and shot her directly in the heart, killing her instantly.

The underling gazed down over at his now-deceased daughter's mother. He knew within a matter of seconds he would die and figured that if he had to go, there was no point in going out cowardly.

"What? Dat 'posed to make me cough up y'all bread 'cause you accidentally killed my B.M.?"

"Blaw!" Jade's gun barked, smashing a slug through the underling's hand and landing one in his scrotum.

"Dumb bitch!" he yelled while rolling over onto his side in pain.

"Uuuhhhmmm," he groaned.

"Don't holla now," Jade yelled.

Kream quickly turned his head as Castro entered the living room clutching two duffel bags that appeared to be overstuffed with five kilos of coke and money.

"Got it . . . let's bungee," Castro stated as he motioned for the door.

Jade's gun barked once more, shooting the Gucci Mane look-a-like in the face as Hysheem dumped several more slugs into his body. Turning her gun to Carla, Jade slowly removed her mask, revealing her identity. Carla couldn't believe her eyes. She stared on in shock for what seemed like forever.

"Surprised?" Jade asked her. "He who deals with anyone is loyal to no one," she continued as she raised her gun, pointing it at Carla's face.

Carla suddenly began pleading for her life. She explained that the Gucci Mane look-a-like on the floor lying motionless was Ya-Yo's little brother and that she was only helping them move work so she could feed her two kids. She also expressed that she was going to enlighten her about the situation and split all the proceeds with her—but Ya-Yo's brother wanted her to keep it internal.

Boc! Boc! Boc! The gun in Jade's hand exploded three times, blasting a hole out the back of Carla's skull. The second shot ripped through her eye socket, as the third splattered her brains onto the couch.

"Treachery is only justified by death," Jade stated calmly.

Satisfied that everyone was dead, they quickly left the apartment, hustling for their vehicles with screaming feet. Once they had reached the stolen vehicles, Castro and Snatch jumped into one, as Jade, Kream, and Hysheem jumped into the other.

"Where to?" Jade asked, stomping the gas pedal to the floorboard.

Young Money answered by informing her of their next destination. Just as they reached the end of the block, three cop cars raced around the corner, dashing by them without a clue they had just passed five ruthless killers destined for the choke of karma.

Moments later, they were pulling into Brier Creek to take care of the other members from Ya-Yo's crew. Kream then exited the vehicle and returned seconds later.

"Castro, come with me," he said, returning to the car. "Keep y'all eyes and ears open," he informed everyone.

Running up the stairs, Kream kicked the door in and rushed inside. He and Castro quickly emptied their guns on all that moved about. They were not concerned with money and drugs. They had showed up to strictly kill—just like real goons.

Hearing a baby crying in the bedroom, Castro entered the room and walked over toward the infant lying on the bed. He then shot the baby in the head, killing the helpless child before rushing out the room.

"Let's move out!" he said to Young Money, breathing hard.

Once outside and back into their vehicles, Kream removed his cell phone and placed two calls, informing two of his Red Diamonds where to meet him so he could pay them what was due to them.

"Fam, I can't believe we bodied nine muthafuckas in less than an hour," Hysheem exclaimed as Jade raced down Capital Blvd.

"Yeah, and one of 'em was my best friend," Jade added. "How could she betray me on such a level so easy?" she asked herself more than she asked her confidants. She was feeling a little guilty and tried to consciously reason with herself but found she couldn't.

"Fuck!" she banged on the steering wheel with her fist.

"Don't stress yourself, Ma. It was justified. She betrayed you . . . now she must suffer da consequences," he said, trying to comfort her.

He then asked for Jade's handgun. Accepting the ratchet from her free hand as she drove, he removed the empty clip and loaded another. Minutes later, they pulled into the parking lot of an old Kroger, then finally spoke.

"I'll only be a minute," he promised. "Gotta handle this one last issue, then we should be cleared," he said before climbing out the car, leaving its passenger door open.

"What it G like, fam?" he stated as he approached the two hood chicks.

"On top of the world," one of the chicks stated, speaking in her ghetto dialect. "Did everything go according to script?"

"Everything, everything," Kream told the chick while turning to face the second chick, "I got something special for y'all," he said.

Kream gazed at the second chick, who looked every inch the haughty in greenish contacts, eye brows waxed to tapered arches, and a mole penciled onto her flawless cheek. However, before she could respond, Kream had yanked Jade's gun free from his waist and shot both chicks dead before they knew what had happened. Once their bodies fell to the ground, he squeezed an additional slug to each chick's head, leaving a mark so that he could recognize them in Hell.

"Bruh, you just gone leave dem bitches like that?" Hysheem asked, eyeing both bodies on the ground through the back window as Jade sped off, with Castro and Snatch following close behind.

"Fuck 'em!" Kream responded calmly. "They were loose ends so I tied 'em. They'll never pull a lil head on me."

"Weak ass nigga," Jade laughed. However, Young Money wasn't in the mood to laugh. His conscious bothered him. He couldn't understand why Castro shot and killed an infant, and knew he would never rest at night until finding out. But first, he had to go clean out Cream's safe.

"Individual character inherits universal honor," Kream whispered, as Jade drove into unknown darkness, heading down 70.

Chapter 9

"It's Showtime"
-Kream-

It was just before 1:00 p.m. when Kream pulled up in his arctic silver over graphite grey-colored Lamborghini Aventador, followed by a fleet of foreign whips. The parking lot was swarmed with some of the phattest stallions on earth. Truckloads, after carloads, of some of the most beautiful, thickest models kept showing up by the dozens.

Tonight's event . . . Tyshineak's birthday bash, hosted by Evelyn Lozada. Ms. Cat was a stand-out amongst them, while Jordin Sparks, Cassie, Rick Ross, P. Diddy, Birdman, and French Montana mingled with the guests. Tony Scott and Messiah also joined the all-star lineup.

Kream, Castro, Snatch, Jade, and about thirty Guardian Angels all stood seductively clad in ZooGang attire, clear-eyed and focused as they trailed Kream to the club entrance. Seconds later, they were accompanied by Hysheem, trailing at least thirty or more Snitch killers behind him. Even Kream's entourage had an entourage.

Once inside the club, they immediately gasped in amazement at its immense size and immaculate surroundings. Club Passion was absolutely gigantic. Rumor had it that it used to be a Walmart. There were four stages and at least 200 dancers.

"Damn, shawty super thick," Snatch said through clenched teeth, turning his head to eye some U-Neak model with European skin and African curves, whose smile matched her sparkly Frankie B. denim that polished off her stylist look from head to toe.

Castro quickly turned around and looked at the European with soulful eyes and a radiant smile as they threaded their way through the crowd of star-studded guests. You could barely move—the place was so packed with too many women. Phat beautiful asses boxed you in everywhere.

"Bruh, shawty do got crazy potential," he agreed, while squeezing through and dancing up on some voluptuous Amazon.

"Bruh, ain't dat chick Ashanti who be in *Straight Stuntin'*?" Snatch stated as she squeezed past him. Seeing her up close, sweaty and naked, had him ready to leave this club shit and go fuck something.

"O, my bad dude," he stated, unconsciously bumping into Fabolous.

Fabolous looked him up and down with a goon-like gaze masking his face. The bottle of Cîroc he had been sipping from spilled all over his color-tee, soaking it.

"Yo, son—watch where the fuck you going," Fabolous yelled at Snatch as Yo Gotti's newest single blasted through the speakers.

Quickly sizing the wannabe studio gangsta up, Snatch looked into Fabolous' eyes and barked, "Dis ain't whatcha want, playboy . . . we just out here trying to have a good time."

"Yo, son—miss me wit' that county bullshit," Fabolous shot back aggressively.

Before Fabolous could utter another word, he suddenly found himself surrounded by fifteen Snitch killers and a statuesque beauty known to all as the numero uno in the streets in Durham: Ms. Jade Parrish. Fabolous tried to maintain his composure and showed no fear, but it was too late—because she had seen right through him.

"Dude, he said excuse me . . . what you trying to pull, a publicity stunt for *TMZ*? If you need some help promoting your next single, get at me," she advised.

"Bruh, this ain't what you want—step before you get stepped on," Young Money comically advised.

Fabolous looked into Kream's eyes, sensing danger, and wisely decided to walk away from the circle of individuals who donned ZooGang attire.

Once he was out of sight, Y.I.P. and family began making their way towards the V.I.P. section, which was reserved for ZooGang. Upon reaching V.I.P., Hysheem noticed a model quarreling with one of the star-tenders about her bill. Without uttering a word, Hysheem reached into his ZooGang denim jeans and pulled out a thick wad of crisp one-hundred-dollar bills and peeled two back with his thumb of the same hand.

"I gotcha, ma . . . it's nothing. Giving is a way of life for me," he paused. "Won't you and your girl come chill wit' a star?"

Without even smiling, the model held her face blank of all expression, slowly stood to her feet seductively-like, pulled her skimpy skirt down, smoothing it with well-manicured hands, and slowly pulled the two bills free from Hysheem's grip.

"Thank you," she stated, making eye contact with him before tucking the two bills into her U-Neak purse.

As he made his way over to accompany his companions on the wraparound couch, two fully naked star-tenders brought over trays of Cîroc and Ace of Spades with sparkles in the bottles shooting off sparks—when suddenly a bevy of U-Neak models began flocking to the V.I.P. section.

"Bruh-bruh, you see something you like?" Young Money murmured into the ear of his childhood friend who had just recently come home from serving time at Polk Youth Institution.

"Shawty, dance for 'em," Kream said to the phat young cutie.

While the curvy French vanilla cutie had his childhood friend preoccupied and tongue-tied, Kream scanned the thousands of patrons for any and all of those who had an intense dislike for him and his family. With observing narrowed eyes, he took note of a league of envious eyes closely watching him and his entourage. Tossing his arm around Jade's neck, he leaned closer to her and asked if she wanted to dance.

Nicely informing him that she had to make a move first, she excused herself and sauntered her way to the ladies' room to return moments later with two small handguns she had strapped to her body before leaving her condo.

"Take this . . . I see we have a lot of juvenile delinquents watching us tonight," she suggested, informing him to extend his hand under the table.

Extending his hand under the table, Kream looked at her with shock in his eyes. He couldn't believe she had taken such a chance. Expecting the small handgun with a smile of approval, he gently cocked a slug into the chamber and tucked the now-loaded pistol into his right pants pocket. Jade then passed the second gun to Castro, as he attempted to stay low in his signature shades, checking to see if anyone had noticed their move.

"It's showtime . . . let's do what we do in a major way," Kream stated, and suddenly everyone began to follow him as he led an exodus of loyal companions through the crowd onto the dance floor.

"Wasted" by Gucci Mane kicked to life through speakers, filtering beats of trap lyrics throughout the club, enveloping everyone with energetic feelings of vibration.

"It's on and popping tonight," DJ Slim Goody started cutting into the music, looking down on Kream and family from the skybox.

"In the building tonight—the Dopeboy King . . . yeah, that's right, the Kream family. And they came out to do what they do best, so get 'cha umbrellas out, 'cause they 'bout to make it rain in this bitch! Young Money, what it do, big homie? I see you, birthday girl—all dolled up, looking supremely seductive!"

Kream and his entire entourage reached into their pockets and backpacks, tossing unlimited bands in the air. The crowd suddenly got unmanageable. Other entourages quickly left their private sections to see what the commotion was all about and gathered around the dance floor to get a closer view of the ZooGang, who had just made history.

Jade, who was having the time of her life with her family—throwing money on a phat young cutie—wore a sensational black leather skirt by U-Neak that set off a figure that made all the U-Neaks in attendance watch her every move enviously, and the dopeboys and celebrities gape.

Kream, who couldn't believe Jade's provocative behavior but found it exciting, was donned out in a collection of ZooGang attire. Wrapped around both wrists sat a chunky diamond time designer and a 254-carat bracelet to match his diamond Y.M.F. and Bentley keychains that flopped around his neck.

Well into the third song by Rick Ross, the crowd continued to stare at Young Money and family as they partied with high feelings of joy. There was no question in anyone's mind concerning whether or not Y.M.F. were the winning circle—for they willingly threw a million dollars.

"I guess we made history tonight, huh?" Jade stated, flashing a huge smile.

"As a movement, yeah . . . but the best is yet to come," he responded as they left the dance floor to join the others. "You and I gone make history once we get to where we going," he challenged, with direct eye contact.

Back on the private balcony after everyone had met back up, the family continued to party like rockstars for hours.

However, every so often Castro, Hysheem, and Snatch would leave the crowded venue to scout seductive models who they observed eyeing them on all occasions.

"Bruh, ain't nothing but star-studded bitches at this star-studded event," Hysheem stated, returning to the couch with two bottles of Ace of Spades in his hand. "Begging to get fucked by us."

Jade was sloshed, and Kream could tell by her actions. All night she had been playing Kream extra close and wouldn't let him out of sight for a second, because she knew the club was overly packed with some of the hottest commodities in the world—waiting for an opportunity to slide in and attempt to seduce Young Money.

"Rich girl, the streets know you a hood fantasy come true, surrounded by global superstars," Kream reassured her with a warm voice. "That's why I choose you to go with me on this special trip. How many street dudes you know can fly out the country on demand?" He smiled.

Slightly off to the right of their table, commotion broke out between two different entourages without warning. Kream reached for his gun but carefully looked around before pulling it out. Upon noticing two security guards breaking the fight up, he could relate as the two were escorted toward the exit door. One of the gang members, clad in sea-blue attire, had approached the other—flamed up in Gucci attire—girlfriend. Jade noticed moments before the verbal altercation had escalated between the two rivals.

Refusing to allow such a disturbance to interfere with their night, Jade and the others kept bottles of Ace of Spades on replay, trying to break a record while blowing money fast—ZooGang style. Purposely, they blew one million dollars.

As the music continued to play and people continued to party, Jade and Young Money continued to converse as if they were in love for the very first time. She asked him so many questions. She wanted to know what island they would be visiting, what surprises would be awaiting her upon their return, and if he was ever going to marry Asia. The only question he answered was the one regarding Asia—by telling her he hadn't decided yet, because someone special had the potential to change his mind while on vacation together. Picking up on his little hint, she laughed heartily.

During their conversation, they both felt as if no one else was in the club but the two of them—when Hysheem walked over toward the couch gripping two bottles of Ace of Spades in both hands.

"Kream," he said with a slight grin. "Shawty over at the bar try'na holla at'cha."

Jade looked into Kream's eyes briefly before he turned to face Hysheem. She was upset by the fact that some chick would disrespect her in such a way.

"What she want?" he asked Hysheem, ignoring Jade's look of contempt.

"A whole thang," he whispered.

Kream couldn't believe that his second-in-command was discussing business in a club, around and with individuals he knew nothing about. Reading into Kream's glance, Hysheem spoke as if he could read minds.

"Shit's official, fam," Hysheem stated while lighting a thick blunt. "Shawty say she connected wit' some official dudes in the industry that you deal wit'."

Young Money raised his eyebrow. "Who?" he asked.

"She wouldn't say . . . said she'll only talk to you."

"Tell them thirsty hoes to fall back," Jade stated sharply.

"Chill, Ma," Kream said, with his eyes on a larger pop prize. As a perceptive observer, Kream could see it all.

"Give me a second," he said as he turned to face Jade.

"You know our motto," she said before he could ask the question.

"More or less!" he responded, before kissing her on her soft bottom lip. "Be right back."

Over at the bar, two extremely beautiful, diversified divas eyed Hysheem and Kream as they pushed their way through the mass of bodies.

"Here he comes, gurl," one of the divas said to the other. "Don't look, 'cause they are looking our way."

"I see," the second diva agreed.

As Kream neared the two divas, he noticed they were seductively dressed in similar catsuits but different colors. Both divas were beautiful, but slightly older than he and Hysheem.

"Excuse me," he softly spoke, approaching one of the two divas, who was currently sitting at the bar sipping from her glass. "You asked to see me?" he questioned, looking the caramel-skinned, toned diva with a flawless face up and down with gangster eyes—but not too thuggish.

Clad in a colorful catsuit with fabric so thin, at first glance he thought he could see through it. At the breast, it fought to restrain Meagan Good-sized tits confined within. Her hair was drama-creating long, stopping slightly below the midsection of her back, and her radiant smile with a full set of lips highlighted the sparkles in her lovely, soft brown eyes in which she told thousands of stories.

Noticing how he looked at her with an intense look, the diversified diva blushed with a smile of satisfaction that he found a plus-size diva supremely seductive to gaze upon. The moment their eyes met, she noticed his pupils quickly dilated—indicating attraction.

"I did," the diversified diva stated with the most seductive voice she could muster. "Can we sit and converse over a drink or two?" she paused. "That's if your companion doesn't mind sharing you a few minutes."

Lifting his hands, Kream smoothly responded, "Do you see a wedding band on my finger?" he asked, as the diamonds around his pinky and wrist illuminated hypnotically.

"Not yet!" she stated, showing off her Colgate smile. "By the way, my name is Shonda Mitchell, and your friend here has told me a lot about you, while getting better acquainted with my sister. And after hearing such wonderful things, I wanted to meet you," she said, extending her hand.

Kream grabbed her soft caramel hand. As his eyes made their way back up to her manicured hand, he found it intriguing how well-toned her legs and arms were. Shonda teased him by slowly crossing her legs in front of him, giving him a peek at her secret opening.

"You like what you see?" she asked sarcastically as she sipped from her Patrón Margarita.

"You hit the gym a lot?"

"Five days a week. I gotta stay in shape in order to maintain this walking billboard."

"It shows," Kream replied, nodding his head in admiration.

She blushed. "Thank you. What about you?"

Kream made a muscle. "I do a lil' something when I can. It's been a minute though."

"Let me see," Shonda said, playfully sneaking a feel on Kream's arm and chest. "You cut up . . . so Malik—" she began.

"Hold up," he interrupted with a raised brow. "How you know my name?"

Shonda looked into his eyes. "Come on now, Malik . . . who doesn't know you? The streets are talking. Besides, I was at your last game against Duke, and unfortunately, I was the one who caught your jersey when you slung it into the stands."

"Kream, so why didn't you come down to the locker room afterwards and let me autograph it?"

"One, because I'm not no groupie. And two, because my intentions were strictly business," Shonda stated.

"How do?" Kream said, gesturing with his hand.

"Well, first off, what was the purpose of you throwing so much money tonight?"

"That's throwaway money . . . what's your point?"

"My point is simple—you could've put better use to that money, like buy into the stock market. That's where the real money at. Y'all need to be playing major league with the white folks. Niggas stagnated when it cost $100,000 on a bracelet," Shonda preached.

Kream took in every word. *Damn, she saying some real shit*, Kream thought to himself before Shonda continued to sow money seeds into his mind.

Shonda looked Kream in the eyes. "Consider the image of a pie cut into a limited number of slices. Each slice represents a share of a C.D.'s stock. If the pie is tasty, and the number of pie lovers is far greater than the slices of pie— then the price of each slice will be quite high, and they will sell quickly. However, if the pie is not very good and/or there are a ton of slices available and very few want it—the pie will be much lower. Both the demand for a C.D.'s stock as well as its availability have an impact on the ultimate price."

"A'ight, I think I follow you. So basically you saying I should look for C.D.'s that are growing their earnings potential?" Kream asked.

"That's the ticket! For example, a C.D. may grow by expanding the number of retail locations, developing a hot new product or technology, or by meeting a new demand in the marketplace. Kream, keep in mind it's not enough to buy the best C.D.'s—you gotta buy the best C.D.'s at the right time," Shonda said as she signaled for the star-tender. The star-tender looked at Kream and smiled when she walked over.

"How can I assist you tonight?" she asked Shonda.

Shonda gave the star-tender and Kream suspicious looks, then said, "Okay, if you don't mind, can you get this seductive young magnet whatever he wants to drink?"

"What would you like to sip on, Kream?" the star-tender asked, Kream grinning from ear to ear.

"Oh, you treating? Well, let me get two bottles on her drink. Here—you may need this." He handed her a napkin, laughing as he did so.

Shonda punched him in the chest as she wiped her mouth. "I wasn't expecting you to order a $400.00 bottle of Spades," she told him.

"Don't worry, Ma, this one on me." He turned to the star-tender headed off to grab the two bottles.

"Ma, I'm curious. Out of all these people out here tonight, why did you choose me?"

Shonda shrugged. "I don't know. Because normally I don't even deal with dope boys, but I like your style and your leadership qualities. Then I heard you were into real estate—that confirmed you were different than a lot of these street dudes out here getting money. Being that you're an investor proved to me that you were a risk taker. If you allow me, I can show you a way to make sure money and even help you clean the money you do have up."

"More or less," Kream said.

"Besides, I figured if I turned you a nice profit, that we would eventually become business partners. I've never been the type to just talk about what I can do—I show you through my actions."

"You the type of person I've been looking for," Kream said as he paid the star-tender for the bottles of Ace of Spades and then poured them a glass.

"Thank you." Shonda grabbed her glass and crossed her legs. The moment her smile left her face, Kream spun around, almost choking on his drink.

"Don't you think you been entertaining this bitch long enough?" Jade barked, with arms folded at the chest while staring at Shonda with a jealous eye. "Looking from afar, this scene looks more personal than business-oriented," she pouted with petulant annoyance in her voice, her bottom lip pushed out.

Not sure how to defuse the situation, Kream killed the last of his drink to steal a moment to make a conscious decision. He then placed the bottle onto the counter.

"Excuse you, but don't you see we're talking?" he finally said with mean eyes that only Jade could read. "What's the problem?"

Remembering how Kream would sometimes function while intoxicated, Jade decided to rattle his cage.

"My problem is with her . . . she knows you're here with me and she all up in your face like I don't exist. How you gone just sit there and let this bitch disrespect me like that, Kream?"

Kream's hand made a slight movement—close to a twitch—and Jade noticed it. She then gazed into Kream's eyes with a laser beam effect and said, "I wish the hell you would," she yelled, sensing he wanted to smack her across the face as he had done before. "Oh, better yet, you can take that bitch with you on your little-ass trip, bastard!" she yelled.

Expeditiously, with the speed of lightning, Shonda slid from the bar stool.

"That's the last time I'ma sit here and let you call me a bitch to my face."

Confronting Jade, she began, "Whatever you two got going on, I don't have nothing to do with it—so keep me out of it. And for the record . . . the only bitch I see acting like a bitch is you," she continued. "Bitch, if you knew better, you'd do better," she advised, before turning to face Kream.

"Malik, I really enjoyed our first encounter. You are definitely a gentleman. Enjoy your vacation . . . call me when you get back in town." She placed the glass on the bar and then reached into her U-Neak purse.

"Here's my card," she told him. "My office number is on the front. Cell number is on the back," she firmly stated before walking off in search of her sister.

Jade, who never got a chance to respond before Shonda abruptly walked off, suddenly felt a little immature and regretted the fact that she had disrespected the woman. She had no idea Kream was conducting business.

"Where you think you going?" he stated, grabbing her by the wrist. "Wit your drunk ass?"

"Let me go . . . go grab that other bitch you had up all in your face."

"Whatever . . . I ain't trying to hear that. Come on, I'm taking you home," he informed her. "You need to rest up, 'cause we leaving for Paris tomorrow."

Jade's body suddenly stiffened. Her eyes grew larger than fifty-cent pieces, and her mouth gaped wide open. She appeared as if she was having difficulty breathing. Screaming at the top of her lungs, she spun, wrapping her arms around Kream's neck, thanking and kissing him with wet lips.

Paris was the one place Jade had always wanted to tour, so Kream figured he would surprise her by making her wish a reality. He then suggested that they leave the club so they could get some needed rest.

"But I gotta see Tyshineak before I leave."

"I can arrange that," he advised.

Peering around the club and unable to find who he was looking for, Kream swiftly made a call, and within seconds Castro, Snatch, and a flock of other members appeared.

"Everything good, bruh-bruh?" Castro asked, sounding out of breath. "Just point 'em out."

Kream, who stood with his arm around Jade's neck, looked them all in the face.

"Nah, everything good. I just wanted to let y'all know we bout to bounce."

"Bark at me tomorrow, fam," Hysheem stated.

"More or less . . . Angel Dust," Kream stated as he and Jade pushed their way through the mass of bodies out the exit door into his Lamborghini.

After he dropped her off at her condo, he headed home to his own bed for the first time in months.

Chapter 10

"Yeah, I'm Prepared to Suffer Da Consequences"
-Castro-

Kream awoke a little after nine o'clock and showered himself under the hot, steamy water. He then dressed down in something casual, nothing expensive; he didn't want to attract the attention of unwanted eyes at the airport. Satisfied with his attire, he reached for his cell phone. Expeditiously, he thumbed the desired number.

"Yo!" A dazed, weak, and unsteady voice sounded in his ear.

"Bruh, you still in the bed?" Kream asked.

"Shit, why not? Your flight ain't until noon."

"Bruh, you sound like you been up all night chasing duckets . . . what time y'all leave the club?"

"Like six . . . me and Roc-Boy left wit' these two bad-ass white bitches from Seattle and got twisted in they dorm. Bruh, Shawty blew my top in front of like seven other bitches."

"So where you at now?"

"Still on campus."

"Well look, I need you to meet me in Knightdale in like a hour, we gotta situation that needs to be addressed before we leave for Paris."

"Say no more . . . I'll be there."

"Angel Dust."

"Say it two times," Castro stated before ending the call.

Reaching across his bedside end table, Kream grabbed a second phone and dialed a series of numbers to some law firm Asia was working at as an intern to gain credits for college. She wasn't due back home until a day before he and Jade would be returning from Paris, which made things better for Kream.

"Hello," a strong male voice answered.

Kream's temperature suddenly soared to its all-time high. *What the fuck some nigga doing with her?* he questioned himself.

"Hello . . ." the voice asked a second time, pulling Kream from his personal thoughts.

"Uh!" he fumbled. "May I speak to Asia please?" he asked, with the gift of mannerism.

"May I ask who's calling?"

What the fuck you mean, who calling? he wanted to shout through the phone but decided against it. "It's Malik."

"Oh, hello Malik, how are you doing? This Asia's uncle Leroy." Recalling he heard many stories about Asia's uncle one night while at her parents' home, his negative thoughts of Asia being with another man vanished.

"I'm good, how 'bout yourself?" Malik asked in a friendly tone.

"Life has been good since I came home from prison. You still playing ball?"

"Not at the moment."

"Well, hold on—here she goes now . . . hold on a minute."

As he waited, he overheard Leroy call out to Asia, informing her that he was on the phone.

"Hey, Bookiebutt," Asia said softly in his ear, with the voice that turned him on the most.

"What's good, First Lady?"

"Everything good, I have no complaints, baby. How about you?" she asked.

"I'm always good, just missing you . . . how was your flight?"

"It was safe, I guess. I slept the whole way here." She paused abruptly.

"What's wrong, baby? Why you sound so down all of a sudden?" Malik asked, noting a sudden change in her voice.

"I'm nervous about going into the courtroom on Monday," she revealed. "I'm afraid I might mess up."

"Babe, stop thinking like that. All you gotta do is stay calm, alert, and be yourself. I got faith in you, you're gonna do just fine," he calmly encouraged her.

"You think so?"

"I know so," he whispered. "But you gotta believe in yourself. You got what it takes, just lean into it," he continued. "Asia, you got what it takes. You're every criminal's dream lawyer, remember that. So when you step foot into that courtroom, remember you're admired by many," he stated, empowering his woman.

"Boy, bye!" she giggled in his ear. "You just trying to boost my confidence."

"No! I'm just playing my role as your man. It's my duty to inspire and empower you," he stated, doing whatever it takes to see his woman achieve her goal.

Malik continued to converse with Asia over the next twenty minutes. Together they shared some unknown fantasies, discussed future plans, and finalized their wedding plan. After ending the call, Malik hit speed dial and phoned Hysheem. He needed a few of his personal business taken care of, and he knew his second-in-command would handle the situation accordingly. Once he received a response from the receiving end, he spoke briefly and confidentially in codes, because he knew there was a slight chance his phone could be tapped.

Disconnecting the call upon completing his conversation, he tossed the device to the bed and began smoking on a blunt of purple flower. Suddenly, he felt light-headed but very well grounded. All kinds of thoughts rushed through his mind. Voices of little children and women could be heard screaming, he saw faces, bloody bodies, and urban-style home invasions and shootouts played over and over in his mind. He suddenly began coughing without warning. Smoke descended from his nostrils like a bull. Trying to control himself and inhale as much smoke as he could in his lungs, he broke out into another fit of coughing.

"Dis shit exclusive!" he suddenly said, eyeing the raspberry blunt as if he was hearing a word from God for the first time.

Looking around the room became complicated for him. He couldn't see anything through the clouded smoke. As the smoke that escaped his lungs only seconds ago rose to the heavens above, his vision slowly cleared. The room's air was filled with thick clouds of smoke he had blown from his lungs like a smokestack pipe.

Two blunts and one shot of Patrón later, he began preparing himself for the meeting he had orchestrated before leaving for Paris. There was a particular situation that transpired under his chain of command that troubled him. The fact that Castro had killed an infant for no apparent reason troubled him strongly. He tried agreeing with the code of the streets—*kill all but infants and small children, but sometimes accidents happen.* However, not in this case, and that is why he couldn't accept the fact that Castro had accidentally pulled the trigger.

Once everyone had arrived at the lounge in Knightdale, they all began forming a circle around the living room by sitting on different sofas. Snatch sat slouched, while smoking a half blunt that dangled between his lips. Jade sat opposite him, smoking lavishly on a blunt, looking over at Castro—who happened to be sipping from a bottle of GTV and smoking chemically coated leaves that are sold in gas stations under the name *Spice.* Hysheem held his eyes high and focused on every hustler in the room. Off to the left in a second room, Roc-Boy sat slouched on a couch in front of an 85" 4K Smart TV watching *The Rise and Fall of F.M.F.*

Kream had been pacing the floor back and forth as the gravity in the room seemed to shift. Chairs were rearranged and a seat was reserved, and Young Money took a load off. Jade handed him a blunt the size of a small baguette, and he sparked it up and reclined like some magisterial hood dope boy.

All heads swiveled toward Kream, who exhaled slowly, letting out a long contrail of smoke. He took off his signature shades, exposing those blood-red eyes.

"Bruh, what possessed you to take out an infant?" Kream suddenly asked Castro. "It wasn't part of the script."

"Why wasn't it?" he challenged.

"'Cause I said it wasn't . . . I feel like you did what you did in hopes to move up in the rank," Kream said while grabbing a magazine. Everyone in the room besides Castro tried to figure out why Kream was speaking so indirect. They knew he didn't like talking in the house; they just couldn't figure out what he was insinuating until he transformed his hand into a gun formation and pointed it at the head of a little boy on the page of an *Essence* magazine.

Jade, who was the first to realize what Kream was insinuating, suddenly glanced over at Castro, locking eyes with his. Instantly, Castro read her mind, and by the time he looked around the room, everyone was eyeing him with faces of stone.

"It was pointless," Kream stated with venom in his voice. "We never carry in that manner . . . that's not how we move."

Castro, unable to find the correct words to explain his actions, peered around the room for some form of understanding. However, all he noticed were displeased faces staring at him.

"Bruh, you said leave no witnesses, so I did what I thought was best at the time," he yelled, while digging into his pants pockets for a pack of Newports. "Don't forget who recruited you. Before us, you was nothing but a schoolboy with hoop dreams."

Deterioration of honor within the family wasn't something Kream stood by. Instead, he was motivated by a strong bond of honor and responsibility toward his family, and he strongly believed the rest of his confidants felt the same as he did.

"Apparently, if you recruited me, you saw something in me that you lack in yourself," he began. "My uncanny ability to produce is why I am where I am. But this meeting isn't about me—it's 'bout you and the bad decisions you been making since the beginning," he stated as he relit his blunt. "Do you even know why you do what you do?"

"I do whatever it takes to win on a good level," Castro stated while exhaling smoke.

"More or less . . . but what goon you know rape bitches and kill innocent kids? Did you know there's consequences behind every deceitful move you make?" Kream stated.

"Yeah, and I'm prepared to suffer da consequences."

"Do that shit bother you?" Jade finally said.

"No doubt," he whispered. "I replay that shit over and over daily, but what's done is done . . . it is what it is—"

"So let's move forward . . . what's done can't be taken back. Bruh made a fucked-up move, but he knows there's consequences behind his actions," Snatch stated before blowing a cloud of smoke toward the ceiling. "Just stay on point, fam."

Silence filled the room for at least three minutes. Snatch, who was the first to speak, reminded everyone of all the good times they'd shared over the years together. As he continued to speak, everyone laughed whole-heartedly as they individually shared tales and jokes with each other. But the mentioning of Carla's name silenced Jade. However, Kream slid onto the sofa beside her, wrapping a comforting arm around her. He then began conversing with her, assuring her that she had done what was best for the team at that particular moment and there was nothing to feel ashamed or guilty about.

Agreeing with him and coming to the conclusion that Carla had betrayed her by entertaining and working with their rival distributing work in Durham city limits, Jade decided never to make mention of such a situation and would continue to do her best to rid her mind of all negative thoughts concerning Carla. Glancing down at her time designer, she informed everyone that it was time for her and Young Money to head to the airport.

"Bruh, you takin' big sis all the way cross country just to smash? . . . it better be worth every stack," Snatch joked with an honest laugh.

"Boo-Boo, it's gon' take more than a trip to Paris to slide between these thighs," Jade shot back. "Besides, it's not all about sex," she lied—knowing exactly what Kream desired second from U.S. currency.

"You ain't said nothing. Bruh got that bread chopped up," Snatch continued while the others loaded the trunk with luggage. "Shit, you fucking wit' a bawse."

"I got'cha, homie," Kream informed him. "You just hold the hood down while I'm gone."

Once the mini yacht had been loaded with their luggage, Jade climbed in, folding herself behind the wheel. "I can't believe I'm only hours away from fulfilling one of my dreams," she said to Hysheem, who was now sitting in the passenger seat just as Kream slid in behind the curtain of his Maybach, closing the door. "I've waited my whole life for this moment." Showing excitement, she spoke as she coasted out the driveway while waving good-bye to Castro and Snatch.

While en route to the airport, the three listened to Jay-Z's latest CD, smoked blunt after blunt, and conversed a little until finally arriving at RDU. Jade pulled into a parking space behind a cab at the curb of the entrance, shut the engine off, and handed the keys to Hysheem, who would be driving the Maybach back to Knightdale.

Moments later, after the luggage had been removed, Kream spoke to his accountability partner briefly concerning his primary responsibility of keeping track of his drivers as they hauled cash and heroin from city to city—and to make sure the couriers got paid and the distributors paid up. Once they both saw eye to eye, they all embraced and saluted one another before departing.

Kream and Jade quietly walked through the busy general aviation terminal on the north side of Raleigh-Durham Airport. The pilots were waiting. They pointed to a handsome little jet parked just outside, ready to take them anywhere they wanted.

Chapter 11

"It All Make Sense Now"
-Lucky-

"This is perfect . . ." the ever-radiant, seductive mistress, dressed in a form-fitting velour sweatsuit with a bouncing bevy of curls, stated to her hairstylist. "I do appreciate what you did to my hair this time," she continued, while checking herself in the mirror. "This color compliments my skin tone, which will allow everyone to focus on my face."

"It really does make you focus more on your face. But that's our brand—we at Hair Estate know the true meaning of reinvention," Terry Toomer responded as she accepted one hundred and fifty dollars from the mistress's hand.

"Where you get those heels from? . . . I like those," she praised.

"These U-Neak?" she stated, lifting her left two-thousand-dollar shoe. "From U-Neak Boutique—Tyshineak just released her signature shoe. Despite what people say about her, when it comes to exclusive designer labels, U-Neak is the place to go . . . You should stop by her shop sometime."

"I think I'll do that. I haven't been to U-Neak Boutique since she was on Chapel Hill Blvd," Terry revealed while admiring the young lady's heels.

"Tyshineak just shut down Raleigh last night for her exclusive birthday bash at Club Passion. Gurl, when I tell you it was a star-studded event, believe me. From start to finish, the club was filled with U-Neak models. Each banner, stand, bucket, and bottle was strategically placed throughout the venue for prime visibility, including a banner at the beginning of the red carpet where the U-Neak models were able to catch celebs as they came in—engaging with the crowd to encourage social media posts and stage product pictures with the celebs. And the ZooGang team did it way too big."

After ending her conversation with the stylist, the seductive mistress exited the salon. Her high heels clicked along the pavement until she reached her Maserati, a gift purchased by a Falcon member. She opened the driver's side door, slid behind the wheel, and started the engine by push button. Pulling out into midday traffic, she checked her sideview; however, she hadn't noticed the ivory-black Range Rover trailing her two cars behind until it was too late.

While pulling into her driveway, she noticed the Range Rover sitting idle, but she couldn't make out the two figures inside from such a distance. The only thing that was obvious was the expensive jewelry they wore, which illuminated under the sunlight above.

Circumspectly, she slid from behind the wheel onto the pavement, wrapped in a yellow fur coat and a Chanel bag draped over her arm, as her free hand snaked inside gripping a baby 9mm handgun Castro had given her for personal protection. Nervously, she tried pretending as if she hadn't noticed the ivory-black Range Rover sitting idle at the curb, while strolling toward the entrance of her mini-mansion in Wakefield Plantation.

"Yo, Joe!" a New York accent exclaimed in a loud, booming voice. "Let me holla at you real quick, Ma."

Spinning on a heel, Joel tried to recognize the New Yorker's face as he walked across the lawn approaching her. The glamorous New Yorker was clad in a sully red fur coat, a pair of G-Star denims, and a pair of Rick Owens sneakers.

However, she took notice of his thuggish swag and quickly came to the conclusion that he was from Harlem.

"I'll only be a minute, Ma," the New Yorker stated, stopping only inches away from her.

"Oh my God," she exclaimed. "You had me all 'noid and shit. What brings you back down South?"

"I'm on assignment, and I need your help."

"What's good, mamie?" Trigger asked, looking Joel up and down as if she was naked.

She looked the thug over. He was draped in red attire, all made by Pelle Pelle.

"Oh, you don't know me now?" he suddenly said. "You been laying low, ain't'cha?" he asked, as if she had committed a crime and now was on the run.

"I don't have a reason to lay low," she responded, opening the door. Once inside the house, she invited the duo into the living room while she left them alone to get something to drink. Trigger took a seat on the sofa as he noticed how expensive every single piece of furniture in the living room was crafted. Everything appeared to be freshly new. He even noticed a few items that could only have been customized in London.

"I asked you a question, but you didn't give me a solid answer."

"A solid answer . . . what you want me to say?" Joel yelled from the kitchen.

"Where you been?"

"Here, there, everywhere, trying to capitalize as much as I can for myself and my brand," she said, making her way back into the living room. "If you want to keep up with me that bad, just follow me on Twitter or find your way on my Facebook. I can't tell you how many times people will read a post and either call, text, or inbox me hollering they can't believe I said whatever. I live life every day and don't mind sharing some of the crazy shit I experience with my followers . . . just send me a friend request."

"Whose crib is this?" Lucky asked.

"It's my castle . . . why?"

"You live here alone?"

The fashion in which the question had been asked raised an alarm in Joel's mind. *Why is he so concerned about whether or not I live alone?* she questioned herself.

"Noooo," she paused. "Me and my dude, why?"

"Who your dude?" Trigger asked aggressively.

"Castro, why?"

"That explains it all," Lucky chimed in.

"What'cha mean?" she asked, sounding sarcastic.

"Exactly what I said," spoke Trigger with sharp eyes of hatred. He then stood from the sofa he had been sitting on and walked across the room to closely examine an 8x10 photo of Joel and Castro walking side by side on a crowded beach out in St. Bart's. "We been looking for you like weeks now. We even stopped by Ceelo's spot in Cary, but whoever came to the door didn't know you. So we figured you went in hiding," he stated, looking around like some private investigator.

"And why would I go into hiding?" she challenged, folding her arms across her chest, somewhat puzzled now.

"So you and ya dude can live life, Shawty, off of Ceelo's expense," he spit at her with conviction in his voice.

The moment such a statement left his lips, it echoed through Joel's ears, igniting resentment, anger, and a rage of silence. She couldn't believe Trigger and Lucky were now accusing her of killing Ceelo for his capital.

"Shit, even a blind man can see what's going on," he added before she could respond.

Joel shot to her feet like a bolt of lightning. "Get the fuck outta my house . . . Now!" she demanded, before spitting directly in his face. "You muthafucking bastard . . . Ceelo was more than my man, he was my soulmate. They don't make enough money for me to betray him. He was my other half, and I would appreciate it if you would respect me as such," she continued, breaking down into tears. "Trigger, you of all people should know how I feel about Ceelo, as much shit as he had me smuggle into a prison for your unappreciative ass," she sobbed.

Trigger wiped his face clean of Joel's spit and set his attention on her for a moment, noticing her violently shaking as if she was about to succumb to a nasty stroke. Viewing how emotional she was, he figured that she was still emotionally attached to Ceelo and gently seated her on the sofa. He revealed to her how sorry he was for not doing his research before accusing her of killing or having Ceelo killed.

"Joel . . ." Lucky finally spoke, kneeling down before her, wiping tears free from her flawless face. He realized at that very moment how beautiful she looked. Her lips were full and accentuated her soft look of beauty that masked her face.

"I feel your pain, Ma . . ." he paused. "It takes a lot to endure the worst of times and still stay grounded during the best of times. But you been able to do so for as long as I can remember," he informed her in a tone barely louder than a whisper.

Calming herself, Joel began framing words to Lucky as if he was a close confidant. She explained to him how Castro and her had met, and how he had been there for her at such a painful and troubling time following Ceelo's death.

"Did son even attempt to find out who killed fam fo' ya?" Trigger asked.

She explained in detail how Castro and his companion started shaking the city in search of Ceelo's killer. She even revealed that after his death, there had been an opening in the North Carolina drug market, and the fact that a lot of hustlers in that field had been shot or killed. She even mistakenly mentioned the fact that Castro and his companions intentionally threw a million dollars at Tyshineak's birthday bash.

"A million dollars . . . Son and dem was eating, but not like that," Lucky stated while pulling on a Newport. "You think Son had something to do with Son's death?"

The moment she tried to voice her opinion, a lump formed in her throat, preventing her from doing so. So she just shook her head from side to side, indicating she had not. Seeing they were getting nowhere, Lucky decided to change his approach.

"Who you know of that was real close to Cee outside of us?" he asked, while gazing into Joel's eyes, hoping to find the truth.

"I don't know, Cee is barely around!" she said, her voice soft and a little raspy.

"You gotta help us put this puzzle together, ma," Trigger advised, using his soft, thuggish accent.

Figuring that Ceelo's minions were very serious, Joel just nodded her head in agreement.

"Look, Ma, what's it gone be? You either gone point us in the right direction or not," Trigger said, serious as a vengeful killer who threatens hood figures. "I'm not gone keep talking though."

Lucky, unsatisfied with Trigger's approach, gave him a look that read *be easy.*

"Well, it's a possibility, but I can't say for sure. But now that you brought it to my attention, I'll look more into it," she suddenly revealed, trying not to say too much too soon because she didn't have any facts to go on. "Give me a few days . . . I'll call you when I know something."

"You know a dude by the name of Kream?" Lucky asked.

"Yeah, that was Ceelo's right hand," she admitted.

"Ceelo's right hand? Then why Cee never introduced him to us?" Lucky questioned.

"Boy, bye . . . You know Malik, the one who played for Carolina?"

"Oh, that's who they call Kream? Yo, son got the whole East Coast chopped up. I never knew Kream was Malik," he continued. "It all makes sense how."

Both workmen couldn't believe what was just revealed to them and looked to one another as if suddenly reading each other's thoughts—both feeling that Kream may be linked to Ceelo's murder. Furthermore, they extended their investigation by maximizing their questions.

Joel revealed unobtrusively and tactfully that she had nothing concrete on ZooGang, but when asked if she knew Zulu, she opened up to them like a novel—explaining to them her real reason for selling Ceelo's estate and why. However, she kept concealed the fact that Castro had killed one of Zulu's hitmen and how she discovered the body in Castro's Chevelle, wrapped in plastic. Nor did she reveal that if Castro and Jade had anything to do with Ceelo's demise, she vowed in silence to slay them both in a unique way.

The moment both workmen left the house, driving off, she fetched her Chanel bag, rumbled through its contents until finding her cell phone. Searching through her contact list for her financial advisor's number, she then hit the send button.

Quickly she instructed her to transfer the 2.5 million Ceelo had left her into a separate account. She then placed a second call to her sister in V.A. She explained to her younger sister all that had transpired within the last four hours and that she strongly believed both workmen had come to kill whoever was responsible for Ceelo's death. She then informed her sister that once she finished school in a few more days, she was leaving North Carolina for good.

Sauntering her way back into the master bedroom after ending the call with her sister, out of curiosity she slid the panel back which led to the closet that hid a safe Castro had installed into the wall—where he hid his money, documents, and jewelry he had recently snatched from a jewelry store in California.

Punching the combination into an assembly of keys, the safe began to register the numbers that had been entered as data into the keyboard. The moment the red light switched to green, she turned its handle and pulled the door open. "Oh my God," she gasped as she looked intently into the safe for the very first time ever. Inside, the safe contained three chrome-plated handguns of some sort, diamonds in all colors, money neatly stacked three feet high from one side to the other, and various documents. Visibly hanging from an AK-47 assault rifle sat a familiar mask. Walking toward it, she lifted it and examined it thoroughly. An awful and foul event from the past flashed through her mind like a bolt of lightning, causing her to tremble and let go of the mask.

"Rich girl," a familiar voice suddenly thundered from the hallway, sounding like Birdman, the CEO of Cash Money.

"Oh shit!" she gasped upon hearing Castro heading her way.

"I figured you hadn't left yet," he lied as he entered the room and found his fiancée relaxing on the bed watching *Colombiana.*

"Come lie beside me," she suggested. She then parted her legs, allowing him to see the print of her secret opening.

Castro bounced onto the bed beside her. "Can we just lay here so I can hold you in my arms?" he said, ever the romantic. "Damn, you smell good."

In all reality, Joel was relieved that she had locked the safe in time. She had made a quick decision to undress in hopes to distract him from seeing the mask lying on the floor.

"You sure that's all you want?" she said, immediately beginning to caress his half-erect dick.

Within seconds, he was fully aroused, which didn't surprise her.

"Hold up real quick," he said, hopping off the bed and vanishing into the bathroom.

She counted to twenty, and he was back.

Taking a seat on the bed, she patted the empty space beside her. "I need you to help me unsolve this mystery."

"It's crazy you say that, 'cause I had the same thing in mind . . . why you got niggaz all in my castle?" he asked unexpectedly, surprising her.

Joel had no idea he knew about the unexpected visit from Trigger and Lucky and was suddenly puzzled by it. *What else did he know?* she thought in silence.

"Who you wit'—me or them?" Castro asked a second time, having received no response to his first question.

"I'm with you, Castro, but I don't like being approached or being in the dark about unsolved mysteries," she responded seriously.

"What unsolved mystery?" he asked with a raised eyebrow.

She quickly explained to him that both workmen were under the impression that they had robbed and murdered Ceelo, then relocated out of fear of retaliation. She also informed him that they strongly felt as if Jade and Young Money played a major role in some way.

"So why they bringing street shit to you for?" he asked. "If they got a problem wit' me, I ain't hard to find. We done cross paths on numerous occasions. If they had a problem with me, they shoulda addressed it then . . . niggas is wacky o."

"Oh yeah? So you mean to tell me you seen them since the funeral and nothing was said regarding Ceelo's death?"

"I mean, shit was said, but not to the extent of me being food. Niggas was more so on some let's-get-money shit."

"So explain the situation with dude in the trunk a couple weeks ago," she stated, knowing he didn't have a clue that she knew about the wrapped body concealed in the trunk of his Chevelle.

"Did Zulu put a bounty out on you?" she revealed, now surprising him.

"That's the word in the streets—"

"That explains it," she interrupted. "Ceelo's people feel like you had something to do with him being killed."

"They can feel how they wanna feel, as long as they don't bring that bullshit my way."

"I don't understand," she paused. "If you ain't got shit to do with it, then why are they sending people out to get at'cha?"

"'Cause they in their feelings right now, but what they got going on, or how they feel about me, ain't none of my business," he stated while pulling off his custom-made Gucci shirt. "I'm about to take a quick shower real quick and meet you in the sheets."

"How about I meet you in the shower instead?" she suggested, unable to resist his fine physique—not to mention his perfect dick.

"That's even better," he said, surprising her.

"After we shower, we going to lock ourselves in this room and have sex for days," she teased, jumping off the bed. "Let's shower . . ." Quick as a flash, she cupped his balls in the palm of her hand. "I'm 'bout to take you to a place you've never been sexually."

Moments later, after their hot romantic shower, they climbed into bed where they began making slow, delicious love. However, while sexing Joel from behind, Castro found himself caught up in a world of endless bliss and pleasure, mumbling something that immediately reminded Joel of the night she had been sexually violated by two masked men. She was having déjà vu.

"What did you just say?" she asked, moving swiftly back and forth on his maleness while looking back over her shoulder.

Castro, suddenly confused, stared into Joel's eyes, realizing an obscured truth of anger he'd never seen before. They were deadly black.

"Dis pussy wetter than a Jacuzzi . . . why, I said something wrong?" he asked, sounding even more confused now. "Damn, yo' pussy stay super wet."

Those exact words had been expressed the night she had been raped. The unsolved mystery had begun to unfold. The ski mask within the safe was also a valuable piece to her puzzle. She was more than sure that Castro was the mystery man whom she so desperately wanted to meet. Maintaining her composure and refusing to tip her hand before its time, she played as if all was USDA certified.

"Oh daddy, deeper," she whispered in her sexiest voice, flashing a beautiful smile that accentuated soft, sheepish eyes.

For two whole years, Joel and Castro went at it like wild animals in heat. She had let him into her heart and allowed him to have his way and sex her in any position he could think of. Energetically, she sexed him back in all attempts to drain him of all the wisdom and power he had in the streets.

"Damn!" Castro gasped, sounding out of breath, as Joel climbed off of him. "Hold up for a minute."

"Mmmmm . . ." she moaned, rubbing his chest. "I'm not done with you yet. I got more work to put in," she informed him, licking cum from his semi-limp maleness.

Before he drifted off to sleep, she questioned him about his trip with Hysheem and Snatch to Miami to pick up five Bentleys, one of which was parked in the garage.

Finally satisfied that he was sound asleep, Joel carefully climbed out of the king-size bed as he snored. She vanished but returned moments later and climbed on top of him as though she was preparing to ride him for the fourth time. She kissed him, which made him wake up—only to find a device that muffled the noise of his .40 cal aimed at his forehead.

Chapter 12

"I'm finally living my dream"
-Kream-

Upon Kream and Jade's arrival in Paris, they excitedly exited the private jet. After gathering their luggage, Jade followed Kream while he headed to grab the rental Maybach he had reserved. Together, after settling down in the Eiffel Tower Hotel, they laid down in bed to sleep off the jet lag they both received from such a long flight. Even though the duo had known one another for such a long time, it was, in fact, the very first time the two had shared a bed together in private. Jade, who appeared slightly timid at first to be sleeping next to her best friend, rolled over on her side and steadily fixed her eyes on those of Young Money. In return, he didn't fall asleep until nearly an hour later.

Awakening early the next morning, they both showered, climbed into the Maybach, and went sightseeing together. First, they drove through and around the streets of France, and Jade was marveled by the gothic and historical buildings and monument structures they passed. She suggested they park the car and do a little shopping. Young Money followed Jade's advice, pulled into a parking deck, and got out. Together they walked the streets hand in hand, looking around at the beautiful scenery and different boutiques before deciding to enter Barney's. Once inside, they spent large sums of money on designer clothing, jewelry, and shades—not only for themselves, but for family and friends as well. Shopping until they couldn't shop anymore, they tossed all the newly purchased belongings into the trunk of their rental before heading to their next destination.

Twenty minutes later, Kream was pulling back up to the hotel. After valet parking, he and Jade headed inside, placed their bags in their room, and headed off to enjoy their evening. Kream had an enchanting evening planned for her. It was a beautiful, windy evening, and the City of Light never looked so beautiful.

The restaurant's parking lot was filled to its maximum capacity when the two arrived. Kream valet parked before climbing out of the rental. With an affectionate arm around the waist of Jade's luscious body, the two clung to each other as they headed inside the establishment.

The romantic atmosphere inside the five-star restaurant was incredible. Everyone looked so important and was well dressed in the latest fashions.

"Mr. and Mrs. Carter," Kream told the hostess with a smile as he approached the podium.

"You made reservations?" she asked, surprised, unaware the reservations had been scheduled weeks in advance. Kream and Jade were led to a table in a secluded area. The hostess handed Kream and Jade menus. He then placed a bottle of champagne from the Château Baccarat collection on the table along with their glasses.

"Would you both care to taste our fine wine of the evening as you take a moment to scan our menu?" he asked before continuing. "Please take as much time as needed; your waitress will be with you shortly." He then excused himself.

Pouring Jade a glass of wine, Kream locked eyes with hers. As he got closer, he was mesmerized by the blackness of her eyes, the long lashes that surrounded them, her glowing skin, and full lush lips.

"Did I tell you how beautiful you look this evening?" he asked, finally pouring himself a glass, still locked into her eyes.

"No, but thank you . . . Malik, please stop looking at me like that before I melt into a big warm puddle in front of all these people," she whispered, licking her lips.

"It's hard not to look at an angel like yourself."

Together they toasted and then politely sipped from their glasses. Kream locked eyes once more, while his mind wandered with thoughts of Jade and how much he wanted her. She was extremely seductive. Her almond-black to almost gold-copper hair was evenly toned, cascading and skimming her shoulders with full, wavy bangs of curls. Her full luscious lips were delicately coated with lip gloss, giving them a look of wetness to the touch. Her flawless butler-brown skin tone highlighted her magnificent eyes and their lashes, affording her such a look she appeared to be a hologram of perfection. She was the perfect woman that God created to be his wife.

Kream couldn't help but stare at her full-sized breasts that desperately tried bursting through the fabric of her blouse that stretched like elastic. Her nipples, far from erect, were visibly noticeable by him.

"What's on your mind, Papi?" she suddenly asked, noticing his lingering stare.

"I was wondering whether or not you had a thong on," he revealed truthfully.

Nonchalantly, Jade sipped wine from her glass without wavering her eyes from his. The moment she removed the glass from her lips she whispered, "In due time you'll know."

Kream suddenly coughed. People all around turned to look in his direction. An alarming amount of blood suddenly rushed to his groin with incredible speed. Saliva formed at the back of his throat; he swallowed hard.

"Damn," he managed to say as she laughed with confidence and control, something he had just lost.

Just as he gained control and was about to speak, the waiter approached their table and took their order. Moments later, order in hand, the waiter cheerfully headed toward

Kream's table to serve him and his guest their evening meal. As if reading one another's thoughts, the duo skipped the à la carte vegetable salad entrée and dessert to jump into the main course. Within a matter of minutes, they both had wolfed their victuals down with incredible speed, like a homeless couple who hadn't eaten in days.

When the bill came, Young Money showed gentleman quality by not looking at the bill and smoothly pulled out his wallet, removed his credit card, and slid it across the table to the waiter, who left and returned seconds later with a receipt and the credit card. Upon retrieving his card, he then tipped the waiter $500.00.

As Malik politely spoke to the waiter, Jade lifted the receipt from the table and quickly, with a curious look, glanced at the bill. Her eyes grew larger the moment she saw the total amount. She damn near gasped in surprise. But instead, she slid it back to its resting spot as she found it, without him noticing what had just transpired.

Out in the parking lot, as their car pulled up in front, Kream opened the passenger side door for Jade, who climbed in with a satisfied smile masking her face. Sitting in silence as he climbed behind the wheel and pulled off, she wondered how he would finish off the night. She stared into his dark eyes and tried to plumb the depths of his soul for answers. She found nothing but more questions.

"You good, Ma?" He lightly touched her shoulder and then quickly withdrew his hand, placing it back on the steering wheel.

"Yeah, I'm good." She paused. "I'm really enjoying this time away with you, Malik," she said, breaking the silence between them. "I've never felt so happy being with someone as I am with you. The whole evening has been a joy to experience."

"I can't recall having a more pleasant time myself," he stated, flashing a huge smile.

"Tonight's event," she searched for the correct words, "will not easily fade from my memory, and my pulse will always quicken with anticipation at the thought of our next rendezvous."

Laughing lightly, he then smiled and glanced her way. "But the night is still young, and I'm not done charming you yet."

"Oh really?" she smiled. "You mean to tell me that there's more in store for me? I can hardly wait, baby," she revealed, looking into the Seine River.

"It's beautiful, isn't it?" he asked, noticing the look of admiration on her face.

"Yeah . . . it's beautiful," she said in amazement.

"You want a closer view on foot?"

Agreeing that she did, he pulled over, parking the car alongside the road where he saw other vehicles lined up. Together they walked hand in hand across the Pont des Arts bridge until finally reaching the sand. After slipping their shoes off, they began to walk along the edge of the sand as the cool water washed ashore, splashing their feet.

Jade was innervated with wonderful feelings of joy. She felt as if she had been newly drawn to him in an inexplicable way. Not only that, but whenever she looked at him, she felt a curious need unraveling inside her. The sun was low in the sky, and people on the Seine River were beginning to pack up and go home. Catching Kream off guard, she bent down, scooped a handful of water, and splashed him, drenching his Burberry jeans. He stiffened in shock.

"Oh, you done started something!" he yelled, splashing her back. "Two can play that game," he said as he splashed her.

Jade screamed and took off running. Malik gave chase; however, Jade was no slow runner. She ran like Gail Devers while yelling, laughing, and screaming like a child at play. Unexpectedly, she tripped and fell into the sand, splashing water. Quickly, she struggled to get back up, but Malik had playfully collapsed onto her. She screamed as she struggled with him, rolling him over onto his back.

"Look who got pinned down now." Scooping water and splashing him about his face, she giggled while sitting on top of him.

He struggled to grab her waist. Her hands moved about wildly, and once he clenched her by the wrist, time suddenly froze without warning. Their eyes met with the intensity of a laser beam. Jade's slight smile quickly disappeared and was replaced by a look of seriousness. Things suddenly began to feel strange. She tried breaking the gaze but found that she couldn't. Communication began taking place beyond her conscious awareness.

Malik's body jerked underneath hers. "Hu . . . ahh," he grunted, clenching his stomach as if he were in pain. "Ummmmm," he cried out as if in agony. Sharp pains suddenly shot through his abdomen.

Jade noticed a look of pain masking his face and stood to her feet. "Baby, are you okay?"

Malik tried to respond. He rolled onto his side and violently vomited. Again he belched. Jade fell to his side in panic. She was ecstatic and frightened, confused, and didn't know what was happening or what to do.

"Baby . . . I . . . need a doctor . . . my stomach is fucked up," he managed to say.

Jade, not knowing what to do, screamed out loud, drawing attention to others in earshot. Quickly, a French woman ran to her side and asked as best as she could what was wrong, in a language Jade couldn't understand. The woman didn't speak English.

A male tourist, who had just arrived, noticed Malik on the ground and asked what the problem was in English. Once Jade informed him, he quickly used his cell phone to call for emergency help, whereupon an ambulance immediately showed up and rushed Malik to the hospital, as Jade followed behind in the Maybach.

For more than three hours Jade paced back and forth across the floor of the hospital waiting room. She had been impatiently waiting to hear from a doctor about Malik's condition and was now becoming frustrated with worry. Knowing there was nothing else to do but wait, she figured she'd call Castro and inform him that Malik was in the hospital. However, she received no answer at his house or on his cell phone. So, she dialed Snatch's number and quickly left a message on his cell phone.

Ten minutes later, she decided to dial Snatch's number again. The moment he answered, she explained Malik's current condition and promised to update him the moment she received any new information. As soon as she ended the call, a doctor walked into the waiting room and asked for her by name. He then explained that Malik had become ill by way of food poisoning and that he'd be fine in a couple of days with a full recovery. Wanting to take him back to the hotel, the doctor advised against it, stating that he wanted to admit Malik as a patient for at least 72 hours and conduct further tests, as well as filter his blood based on the fact that the poison had entered his bloodstream.

For the next three days, Jade's life had become a living hell. She felt so lonely and lost without Malik. She only felt better when at his bedside, talking to him. But through it all, she remained strong and firm, even though she hated seeing him hooked to so many tubes that snaked to different machines. Deep in her heart she knew it was best for him.

Finally, the morning she thought would never come arrived. Malik was released from the hospital with an excellent bill of health. Jade was nothing but smiles and fully consumed with pure happiness.

"Papi, you know we only have one day left in Paris, right?" she reminded him as they climbed into the rental Maybach. "So I prepared something special for you."

"Oh yeah?" he asked softly. "I just hope we're not eating out again, cause I'm not eating none of this shit out here again."

Silence filled the car as Jade drove through the busy streets, giving thought to Malik's statement. However, the surprise she had in store for him had nothing to do with food. In fact, she figured it would be best if they picked up where they left off. So, for the remainder of their drive, they casually held conversation until they reached the hotel.

"Okay, close your eyes," Jade instructed Malik as they opened the door. "I got a surprise for you, Papi."

Slightly confused, he locked eyes with Jade as if he could read her thoughts. Seconds later he spoke. "Jade, watcha up to?"

She kissed him on the lips quickly, pulling him back. "If I told you, it wouldn't be a surprise, now would it?"

He shrugged. "It depends."

"Boy, close your eyes and let me do what I do best." She pouted, a seductive gaze upon her face.

Closing his eyes, Jade opened the door and guided him inside, locking it behind them. She looked intently around, carefully checking the room to ensure everything was in its proper place. Satisfied with what she saw, she led him to a nearby sofa where he took a seat.

"Keep them closed a few more seconds . . . and don't look."

"So this is what it's like to walk in Stevie Wonder's shoes?" he joked. "How much longer do I gotta play Stevie?"

"Just a few more seconds, babe . . . a few more seconds," she grunted, sounding as if she was at work or something.

Hearing what sounded like clothing snapping and popping, Malik fought the urge to open his eyes. "Ma, watcha up to?" he curiously asked. "I feel like you tryna steal my soul."

Feeling Jade climb onto the sofa beside him, he attempted to turn his head; however, she whispered in his ear just as *Sent from Heaven* by Keyshia Cole filtered through the speakers, filling the room.

"I don't want to steal anything from you . . . I want to give you something. Please, just relax," she said in a seductive soft voice. "Stick your tongue out," she ordered.

He stuck out his long pink tongue, and she leaned forward so that he could lick on her dark nipples.

The room had been darkened by closed curtains. Twelve candles provided a soft glow of romance as the flames gently danced in shadow form against surrounding walls. Rose petals covered the floor, leading to a trail down the hall into the master bedroom.

Malik, amazed by what he saw, stared in silence as if his eyes were having an intense orgasm. Shifting to say something to Jade, he suddenly gasped in amazement. Jade stood slightly to the side. A swell had somehow formed between her legs, giving off a perfect V-shape in its most glorious state.

"Damn," he gasped, sounding damn near breathless. "I'm finally living my dream," he mumbled as all the blood within his body rushed to the tip of his maleness.

"Shhh." Kneeling to the floor between his legs, she hushed him as she began removing his clothing. She grinned and looked happily at his sex. It stuck up between his muscular thighs like a blunt hammer. He noticed for the first time that he was uncircumcised. She didn't know many uncircumcised men. Curious, she placed her hands on his knees and made a place for herself between his thighs.

"I might as well introduce myself to the royal penis," she thought to herself. It was swollen and stiff, and the prominent vein on his maleness was throbbing.

She moved closer to see the bubble forming on the tiny lips, and in doing so, she bathed the thick head with her warm breath. She licked delicately at it, the tip of her tongue investigating the folds of the warm skin. She slowly sucked its imposing length between her lips, savoring the salty fluid that seeped forth to flavor her tongue. She folded herself between his legs gracefully, like a dryad, like a princess, and sipped tenderly at his flower.

Finding it very difficult to speak in such a position, all Malik could do was take deep breaths in order to control his excitement as she applied stimulating feelings of pleasure, like a high-class whore. Her hands moved up and down his muscular legs, rubbing, caressing, pulling his need from him. Her long neck bent swan-like to the present task of teasing him beyond endurance, so that Malik would give up his long-stored cream to her. His leg moved weakly as if to escape from Jade's hot, enclosing mouth.

"Ummm," he moaned just as Jade moved her head back and forth on the maleness flowering in her mouth.

When Malik began to roll his hips, to force himself deeper into her face, Jade encouraged his thrust by pushing one slow finger into the muscular ring of his anus. Lost in the heat of her excitement, she was anxious to fill herself with him, to swallow him, to consume him. Her fingernails raked his chest.

Nearly an hour passed since Jade had started performing her little trick on Malik. Just as he was about to cum, he grabbed the back of her neck and tried ramming his sex down her throat deeper to deliver his seed. However, just as she had been doing all along, she stopped. She didn't want him to explode just yet. She wanted to give him so much pleasure that he would never forget this romantic setting with her.

She looked at his face without surrendering his flesh and saw that he was biting his lip. Malik felt as if his testicles would explode without warning. He threw his head back, shut his eyes, and moaned rhythmically. Jade moved his hips easily with one finger inside his body and made them roll forward so that she could stuff more of him into her throat. The heavy glans on her tongue throbbed and fluttered against the roof of her mouth, warning her that soon it would boil over. Jade swallowed and relaxed her lips.

Malik couldn't understand why she kept preventing him from cumming. However, he had no idea that Jade was the kind of diva who, when hot and aroused, needed to be sexed for hours until she was completely exhausted and sexually drained.

"Come on, baby . . ." she said, pulling him slowly from the couch by one hand, leading him up the spiral stairs to the master bedroom. "You got me so fucking horny, Papi." She spoke aggressively with lust in her eyes.

Grabbing her by the waist, Malik gently pushed her to the floor, spreading her legs.

"Ohh nooo . . . not here, Papi . . ." she tried speaking. However, he ignored such a panting protest and slowly pulled her thong down, glancing between her slightly parted thighs as she raised her derriere from the floor to help remove it. The thong slightly snapped away from in between her inner secret opening.

Spreading her thighs ever so widely, she started talking dirty to him in Spanish, knowing it turned him on. Jade was full of sensual attitude and between her legs wetness seeped from her inner cuntal lips like clam juices. A burning fire reared in her body. She needed him, wanted him, and the pleasure she had received from sucking his swollen flesh was like a wild burning flame that only he could put out. "Ssss!" she whispered a hiss of lust and jumped—sucking air in between clenched teeth the moment his tongue flickered at her erect nipple, while simultaneously slipping a finger in her hot wet opening to his knuckle. "Owww!" she cried slowly as he brushed his finger gently across her clitoris, moving up and down, in and out, sucking on her nipple at the same time.

She quivered from such a sensation. Her stomach rolled and fluttered as her breathing became heavier. She felt breathless and couldn't believe the strength he possessed and the will to take his time. The fact that he was in complete control frightened her a little, but she was looking forward to such a thrill, knowing he had never eaten pussy—or so she thought.

Jade slithered around her body. She flinched when she felt his warm mouth on her clit. It was amazing how he knew her body better than she did. "Oh, Papi . . . shit, you feel so damn good!" Jade moaned, rubbing his head.

Gently sliding two fingers in her now extremely wet opening, Malik used them to spread her inner darkened pussy lips, and with his other hand, he pushed the skin back on her hooded clit. He then began flickering his tongue in and out, up and down, deep within the walls of her secret opening and against her clit with thug-passionate skills.

"Oh . . . my God . . ." she jumped and gasped, slightly bending her knees. She attempted to lift her rectum from the floor but found she couldn't. "Oh . . . yes . . . yes . . . ohhh. Ooowww, God," she continued to moan.

As he relentlessly lapped away at her dripping wet cunt, her lips engorged and swelled two times bigger than normal. Such a sensation drove her wild and far beyond the point of crazy. The desire and sensation were too intense. She tried pushing him away, squirming like a fish out of water, but Malik instantly clamped down on her clit, locking it between his lips.

Now that he had her where he always wanted her, he struck at her clit with a serpent tongue, then back and forth across its nerve endings like a licking lizard.

"Oh, Malik," she bellowed in the process of cumming. "Ummm . . . uhhh . . . ahh . . . yess . . . yess." She rolled her hips as she suddenly began yelling in a high-pitched tone of voice, gasping uncontrollably.

"Damn, oh shit, ple . . . pl . . . please . . . oh, Malik, I need you inside of me," she begged, tossing her hands out to the side as her head rolled from side to side. She dug her nails into the fur carpet like cat claws. The look of pain mixed with intense pleasure masked her face. "Oh, Malik," she gasped for air. "S . . . I'm cumming . . ."

Electricity shot through her body, her legs suddenly went stiff, and her whole body locked. Suddenly there was an explosion between her legs like she had never felt before. "Owww . . . ssahhh . . . mmm." She grunted hard as her stomach muscles clamped and locked, as if she was pushing a baby free. Her entire body felt as if it was locking under her eyelids. Her toes curled backwards, popping at the joints, and for a split second she felt as if she had lost consciousness and touch with all reality.

"Oh, Malik," she panted in all attempts to catch her breath. "Damn, your head game official," she puffed.

Unable to believe how hard she had come, she lay motionless on the carpet, feeling as if her clit wouldn't stop tingling or throbbing. Slightly she touched it with her finger. "Ssss . . . ooowww!" she moaned.

"Let's take this show to the bedroom, Ma," Malik finally said, a signature smile masking his face.

"What's so funny?" Jade asked, noticing his smile.

"You and them faces you be making when I be putting my super head game down," he joked.

He took Jade's hand and helped her to her feet. They made their way to the bedroom, and once inside, she laid across the bed on her back, slightly spreading her legs, knees bent. She then grabbed both titties and began flicking at each nipple with her tongue tip, enhancing and inspiring Malik to take her immediately. She wanted to be ravished with brute force. She had never felt so horny in her life.

Positioning himself over Jade in a push-up position, with hands alongside her body, he looked into her eyes, scrutinizing her face, noticing a mask of pleasure beckoning him to enter her wet folds. Sensing a hint of shyness in his eyes, she reached between her legs and firmly wrapped her fingers around the stone pillar of his sex. He was massive—large, she thought in silence. Summoning the courage to take him, she willed all apprehensive thoughts from her mind and slowly guided the tip of his head to the entrance of her love, spreading her legs slightly wider.

Grasping from her warm fingers, he slowly pushed his swollen flesh forward as its tip parted her secret opening slightly. She arched her lips, raising her derriere from the bed, and gasped as a lightning bolt shock ripped through her cunt lips. She felt as if he had ripped her.

Just as her body twitched, he pulled back, positioning himself to hold his weight on one hand. He gripped his stiff flesh with his free hand just as she turned him loose and began sliding the head of his thick penis down the length of her entrance, smearing her juices as if it were petroleum jelly between her legs for lubrication. "Mmmm," he moaned, loving the sensation and warmth she gave off.

Seconds later he mashed forward. She felt incredibly tight but soon loosened to accommodate him. Slowly he traveled forward until he had completely entered her to the hilt.

"Owww," she gasped, trying to slide back to get away from the pain she felt deep at the bottom of her walls. Her insides tingled with fire as he slowly worked inside and out.

"Oh, Malik, you da bawse . . ." she whispered over and over, clawing his back with fingernails, drawing blood. Slowly, she began grinding her hips to meet his thrust.

"Let's take this show to the bedroom, Ma," Malik finally said with a signature smile masking his face.

"What's so funny?" Jade asked, noticing his smile.

"You and dem faces you be making when I be putting my super head game down," he joked.

He took Jade's hand and helped her to her feet. They made their way to the bedroom and, once inside, she laid across the bed on her back, slightly spreading her legs, knees bent. She then grabbed both titties and began flicking at each nipple with her tongue tip, enhancing and inspiring Malik to take her immediately. She wanted to be ravished with brute force. She had never felt so horny in her life.

Positioning himself over Jade in a push-up position, with hands alongside her body, he looked into her eyes, scrutinizing her face, noticing a mask of pleasure beckoning him to enter her wet folds. Sensing a hint of shyness in his eyes, she reached between her legs and firmly wrapped her fingers around the stone pillar of his sex. He was massive—large, she thought in silence. Summoning the courage to take him, she willed all apprehensive thoughts from her mind and slowly guided the tip of his head to the entrance of her love, while spreading her legs slightly wider.

Grasping from her warm fingers, he slowly pushed his swollen flesh forward as its tip parted her secret opening slightly. She arched her lips, raising her derriere from the bed, and gasped as a lightning-bolt shock ripped through her cunt lips. She felt as if he had ripped her.

Just as her body twitched, he pulled back, positioning himself to hold his weight on one hand. He gripped his stiff flesh with his free hand just as she turned him loose and began sliding the head of his thick penis down the length of her entrance, smearing her juices as if it were petroleum jelly between her legs for lubrication.

"Mmmm," he moaned, loving the sensation and warmth she gave off.

Seconds later he mashed forward. She felt incredibly tight but soon loosened to accommodate him. Slowly he traveled forward until he had completely entered her to the hilt.

"Owww," she gasped, trying to slide back to get away from the pain she felt deep at the bottom of her walls. Her insides tingled with fire as he slowly worked himself inside and out.

"Oh, Malik, you da bawse . . ." she whispered over and over, clawing his back with fingernails, drawing blood. Slowly, she began grinding her hips to meet his thrust.

"Oh, Malik . . . mmmm . . . ahh, yess . . ." she gasped in his ear while caressing his back softly. She couldn't believe how awesome he felt inside her. Wrapping her legs about his waist, locking them at the ankles, she began grinding anxiously to orgasm.

Locking eyes with one another, with love, lust, pain, and pleasure masking their faces, they began pounding with matched rhythm and loud grunting sounds.

"Damn, this pussy good. Can I cum in you?"

"Please do, give me all you got," she begged.

Suddenly he gripped her legs underneath the kneecaps, pushed her legs all the way back and wide open, and, raised on his toes, began long-dicking her. He drove deep within her walls, ramming forward over and over, in all attempts to give her the fucking of her life.

"Ahh . . . ahhh . . . ahh . . ." she grunted with eyes closed as oh-so-good electricity shot through her body, tingling every nerve ending within her sex. She couldn't hold out in such a position any longer.

Loudly they both began grunting and yelling as the headboard banged and pounded against the wall, adding to their loud noise. Jade began screaming that she was about to cum, and Malik began pounding into her harder. The moment she began clamping down on his maleness, he too felt his orgasm building. She sensed he was about to cum, pushed him off of her after having cum, and kneeled before him, taking his swollen stiffness into her mouth.

"Ummm," he grunted loudly, as the thick, salty nectar pumped from his exploding sex in an endless hot stream. "Uhhh . . . ahhh . . ." he grunted with a mighty strain as Jade swallowed as fast as she could, the excess rolling down her chin into her breasts.

Shifting his position, he then quickly shoved his maleness in between Jade's ass cheeks and entered her rectum. She dropped on the bed, derriere up, and grunted as he began dipping in and out of her hot love.

After nearly four songs later in such position, her breathing began to change with each stroke he took.

Suddenly her secret opening throbbed with sensations as she began rubbing her clit towards orgasm.

"Ahh . . . I'm 'bout to . . . ahh . . . cum . . . faster, Papi . . . faster, muthafucker . . . oh God, this dick feels so good!" she yelled as they both came together, semi-conscious to the world and clasping to the bed.

"Hmmmmm . . ." said Jade, sitting up in bed and stretching for a pillow. "Now I see why Rachel always complains."

"Shit, what she got to complain about?" asked Malik, reaching across her full breast for a blunt and lighting up. He took a few pulls before passing it to Jade.

Jade drew deeply on the blunt. "Your . . . er . . . enthusiasm, stamina, and staying power."

"So you telling me, y'all be sitting around talking about me?"

"What else is there to talk about?" She lifted one leg from beneath the sheet and trailed her toes down his chest. "You . . ." she murmured huskily, "go hard for yours. And I . . . go super hard for mines. You ready to go another round? I didn't fly out here to talk."

He lifted her toes to his mouth and sucked on them one by one. "Who's talking?" he growled.

Chapter 13

"No witness…No case"
-Joel-

Having returned home, Kream and Jade greeted Snatch and Hysheem in the airport parking lot with warm smiles and hugs. However, even though both hood generals held vibrant smiles across their faces, Young Money immediately sensed something wrong and pulled Hysheem to the side for a private discussion.

His second-in-command quickly but briefly informed him that Lucky and Trigger had been in town asking a lot of questions about him and Jade concerning the home invasion that led to Ceelo's death. He also brought to light that Castro had been missing since the day they returned from Miami, and the fact that they had searched every stash house and spoken with every one of his chicks concerning his whereabouts but hadn't received nothing concrete.

Suggesting that they place their luggage in the trunk of Snatch's Bentley and drop Jade off at her condo so they could discuss the issues at hand in private, they walked over to their cars to join Jade and Snatch. Quickly, they tossed their entire luggage into the trunk and folded themselves behind the wheel. Snatch and Hysheem had paired up in his car, while Jade and Kream paired up in the car that Snatch had driven to the airport. Just as they pulled into traffic, a blue BMW trailed them from behind at a safe distance.

"So you enjoyed yourself?" Kream asked Jade, who now sat on the passenger side with her head slouched in the cushion headrest, eyes closed.

"I did . . ." she simply responded without opening her eyes, "especially our last two days together locked away in our room. You actually took me to a place that I've never been sexually." She revealed with a full smile masking her face, turning her head ever so slightly. She peered downward, hit a button, and lowered her window about two inches. "How about you? Was it as adventurous to you as it was to me?"

Maintaining silence a moment, he thought about what had been said. "No question," he yelled. "Shit, we made history."

Jade hit him in the chest, catching him off guard. "I'm not talking about the trip within itself," she giggled. "I'm talking about our time together in bed, silly—don't play."

He laughed lightheartedly, then spoke. "Each moment spent with you, to me, is special. What we have excels all other relationships I'm currently in."

Shifting her seat to face him with a smile, she looked him about the face and said, "You really mean that, Kream?" He nodded his head yes. "I feel the same way, you long-winded, stamina-filled young muthafucka." She laughed. "You got my pussy extra sore, Papi . . . gosh—I've never came so many times in one night." She confessed as she reflected back to the shower scene that transpired this morning, wishing she was still living in the moment.

Forty-five minutes later, they pulled into the brick, climbed from their cars, unloaded both vehicles, and carried their luggage and gifts inside.

"Jay . . ." Kream unexpectedly called out to Jade, dropping the large-size teddy he had won at a carnival event on the sofa. "Come here real quick, let me show you something before I bounce. You are going to love this," he assured her.

Jade looked him in the eyes with a puzzling gaze masking her face. She then took his extended hand and walked with him through the living room, down the hall, and through the kitchen as Snatch and Hysheem followed close behind.

Reaching the door that led into the garage, Kream informed Jade to close her eyes. Guiding her down the steps carefully into a small circle, he told her to open her eyes.

Dropping her hands to her side, she gasped from shock and looked around, her mouth held wide open. She tried to express herself verbally but found it difficult. She couldn't believe Kream had actually purchased her dream car.

Shifting her gaze back at the passion-pink metallic Bentley GTC, she gasped a second time before racing to its side, sticking her arm through the passenger-side window, and looking around in amazement. Luxuriously outfitted, inlaid interior piping lined its seats, doors, and dashboard, elevating its inside lavishly. The word *Jade* had been stenciled within the headrest of the front and back seats. Black carpet covered the floor, and four DVD-TV screens had been positioned before each seat, lowered from the ceiling.

"Ahhh!" she suddenly started screaming before pulling her head from the window. Her screaming continued as she stomped while spinning in circles. She then jumped into Kream's arms, hugging him about the neck lightly as she wrapped her legs around his waist.

"Malik, oh my God . . . Malik . . . thank you . . . thank you," she cried with joy over and over. Kream struggled to remain standing as Jade bounced up and down about his body. He fought hard not to drop her, and when she had finally calmed down, Kream asked if she liked it. She responded by thanking him again and once more for the Giovanna rims and the personalized license plate that read *Rich Girl*.

"I copped Castro and Hysheem the most expertly appointed Bentley Mulsanne as well," he shared with her. "I told you, in two years the whole team would be pushing Continentals."

Jade, touched by his token of affection, asked him to stay the night, but he politely declined, informing her that he needed to get home and meditate.

Accordingly, they all entered her mini-mansion and spoke for a few until Hysheem took notice of his Bentley timepiece, realizing it was nearing midnight.

Once out front near their exclusive toys, Kream called both hood generals over to his car. He was puzzled by Castro's sudden disappearance. "So when was the last time you hollered at bruh?" he asked Snatch.

"The day that he followed me out here to park Jade's car. He was talking like he needed a break and was considering whether he was gon' fly out to Vegas or Dallas."

Kream thought in silence for a moment before speaking. Castro was not the type to just up and leave town without informing him or Snatch, and that statement alone was now puzzling him greatly.

"Did you swing by Joel's and pick her brain?" he asked.

"Like two hours ago, but no one came to the door. But when I looked in the garage, all of his toys were there," Hysheem admitted.

"Some'em ain't right . . . Snatch, you did say bruh was driving the Bentley when you last saw him, right?" Kream asked with a strained voice, attempting to make sense of it all. Snatch nodded in agreement. "Anybody seen Joel?"

"Nah, shawty missing too," Hysheem added. "Maybe they left together in her car."

Kream suggested that they ride out to Castro's estate and investigate the matter further. Both generals agreed, and just as they were about to climb in their vehicles, Snatch's phone rang. Snatch answered, then paused. "Yeah, bruh right here . . . hold up." He said this while looking over at Kream with a puzzled gaze wrapping his face.

"Who the fuck calling yo' phone for me?" Kream asked, reaching for the phone.

Snatch shrugged, showing he had no clue.

"Talk," Kream thuggishly stated.

"Red Rum Salute . . ." a female voice stated through the phone. "From my understanding, you are looking for a rapist, right?" the diva said more than asked, speaking indirectly concerning a situation of great significance.

Although Kream was extremely conversant in street lingo and insightful in his own way, he had no clue what the young diva was trying to insinuate, so he considered his thoughts before voicing his opinion. Recognizing her voice, he decided against calling out her name.

"Shawty, what'cha got going on?" he finally said, momentarily looking over at Snatch and Hysheem.

"Whatever you do, don't mention my name on this phone, 'cause there's a slight chance your shit might be tapped," the voice quickly interrupted. "But anyway, that trash you looking for is in the garage. I got approached a few days ago, and after what was said, I connected a few dots which ended in blood."

"So what's really good?" he questioned, not wanting to say too much over the phone.

"Just check the garage out and everything I've said will come back to you. And let Snatch and Jade know when I see 'em it's Red Rum on sight." As she continued to reveal all of the facts, Kream quickly realized what had transpired and remained silent just in case Snatch's phone was tapped—he wouldn't incriminate himself.

"Oh, and one more thing, Kream." There was a pause. "It's a bitch in your circle that's working with the feds. If I'd known beforehand, I would have told you, but it just recently fell in my lap. Anyways, she has a file on you, mostly photos and reports, nothing concrete . . . my advice to you . . . no witness, no case—"

"Why you telling me all this?" he asked, interrupting her, wanting to know why she was revealing such information to him.

"For two reasons . . ." there was a pause. "One, because this bitch only befriended me to fuck and build a case on my man. And secondly, you didn't play a role in violating me . . . 'nough said . . . Angel Dust."

Slowly pulling the phone from his ear with a look of bewilderment wrapping his face tightly, he handed the device back to Snatch. Briefly, he explained to his confidants the contents of the call and who was behind what they supposedly would find in the garage. They quickly mounted up and raced towards Castro's mini-mansion to investigate what Joel had spoken indirectly about. Finally reaching the sleek mini-mansion, they entered the garage cautiously while looking around wildly. From someplace within, a foul stench immediately assaulted their nostrils with a murderous, fetid, and decaying odor.

"Ahhh . . . man . . . what the fuck is that smell?" Snatch barked, grabbing his nose with clenched fingers it's the worst.

"Damn!" Hysheem agreed, holding his breath.

With frightening thoughts, Kream spotted Castro's keys dangling from the trunk of the Bentley after hitting the lights. He then informed both hood generals not to touch anything unclothed because the smell that was in the air was probably coming from Castro's body.

Slowly he approached the trunk, and the closer he got, the stronger the smell became. Using his shirt, he turned the key and jumped upon discovering Castro with his balls stuffed in his mouth, his last meal before dying.

"Ahh man, damn, Castro!" he yelled out loudly.

They all looked into the trunk with mourning eyes. The upper part of Castro's face was covered with the same ski mask he had worn when he raped Joel, and his body lay stiff on top of a sheet, covered with maggots and flies that feasted away at his flesh.

"Damn, she cut his balls off and stuffed 'em in his mouth," Snatch breathed.

"She had to catch him while he was sleep," added Young Money.

"What we gone do with his body?" asked Hysheem. "We just can't leave bruh laying like this." He spoke truthfully.

Snatch and Hysheem turned to face Kream for advice, and at that very moment silence filled the space between them. Neither general knew what to do, but there was no way possible they would leave their companion in such a position. They also knew that if the police got a whiff of the body, an investigation would follow that could possibly unearth all the dirt within their past.

Kream stepped back from the car and walked in a small circle, taking a moment to think things out in silence. He figured that Lucky and Trigger must have played a role in Castro's death. However, what he couldn't understand was why both goons would leave his body behind, because they were too experienced for such a sloppy move.

"Bruh, you think this some of Lucky and Trigger's work?" Kream suddenly spun, asking his confidants.

"Nah, ain't no way," Hysheem replied. "Bruh stayed too on point to slip like that. This looks like some after-sex solo project. Joel's the only one who could have gotten that close to take bruh so easily."

"More or less," Young Money said.

"Bruh . . ." Snatch suddenly said. "You think she had access to his safe?"

Quickly, the three generals scrambled into the house en route to his safe.

"Damn, she extorted bruh for all his treasures," Kream said. "Guns and all . . . sheisty bitch." He screamed out loudly. "If I ever see that slut, I'm going to kill her myself."

"That's the plan . . ." Hysheem spoke, looking at the blood splattered on the pillow. "But what we gone do with his body? The sun 'bout to come up and nosey neighbors gone be curious why so many cars out front, and I ain't tryna get my shit hot . . . ya smell me?"

"We gonna bury 'em."

Silence filled the room as they thought. "Fuck it . . . let's do what it do and handle it."

"More or less . . . then we gotta go and handle Des," Kream swore.

Having come up with a better solution, Hysheem glanced over into Kream's eyes. "I got a better idea, fam—how about we grab shawty and bury her too? That way we kill two birds with one stone."

Snatch and Kream agreed it was a good idea before heading back to the garage after finding a box of latex gloves. Having decided who would drive which car, they all carefully coasted off into the morning fog towards Destiny's house.

As Kream drove in silence, he thought back on all that he'd been through, and the one thing that troubled him the most was the fact that he couldn't foresee Destiny being a federal agent. The more he thought about it, the angrier he became. He even cursed himself for slipping and not listening to Asia. She had warned him that the feds were probably watching him closely. But he would have never figured it would be Destiny to take him down. In one way or another, he felt as if he would be in forever debt to Joel because she had enlightened him with such confidential information.

Finally reaching Destiny's house in the upscale Raleigh suburb, he pulled alongside the curb, climbed out, and had a few words with Snatch and Hysheem before knocking on the door.

"Yes?" a lovely voice answered from the other side of the door moments later.

"It's me. Open up," he said calmly.

Locks clinkered on the door before it opened. "Hey, sweetheart . . ." Destiny said, eyeing him with an exotic gaze. "How was Miami?" she asked, spinning around on her running shoes as though she was prepared to go for a jog.

Snatch and Hysheem burst into the house like a gust of wind the moment Kream broke the threshold. Both hood generals held silent Glocks in their hands, trained on their intended target.

Hearing the sound of clattering boots, Destiny quickly spun around to face her intruders. "What's going on, Malik?" she asked in shock.

Maintaining his silence, Young Money approached her, looked into her soulful eyes, and with the speed of lightning he spit a razor from his mouth, ending her constant whispering with the whisper of steel passing through her neck.

"Bitch, you knew the rules . . . you played a very dangerous game—and you lost," Kream expressed. "Now let's go find Lucky and Trigger."

Chapter 14

-Please Don't Go."
-Asia-

For the next two weeks, all had been quiet in the Bull City. Kream and his guardian angels had been searching high and low for Lucky and Trigger. Kream figured that once Destiny's disappearance made CBS Evening News with Scott Pelley—informing the public that she was an FBI agent who had been working an ongoing investigation for the past three years—Ceelo's minions cowardly left the city. Since they were nowhere to be found, Hysheem suggested that Asia have her own personal bodyguard to protect her until the duo could be found and dealt with. Young Money agreed with him and hired a twenty-four-year-old diva by the name of Lakeka Pulliam, a.k.a. Spandora, to watch over Asia until he and Hysheem got rid of the kilos they had left in the stash.

Spandora was an extremely beautiful woman who had spent six years in the United States Marines as a weapons specialist. She stood six feet even with a perfect six-eight frame. Her jet-black hair, which she wore short and curly, accentuated her flawless pecan-brown face and almond-shaped brown eyes. She appeared to all as beautiful, but in plain truth, she was more deadly than any woman the streets of Durham had seen or come across.

As if old friends, she and Asia hit it off very well and had become good friends within a short time. Together, the pair had spent countless hours, and even though Spandora followed Asia every step—no matter where she went—Asia enjoyed her company and the different points of view she had on life.

Slowly pulling alongside the curb in front of Hair Estate Salon, Spandora parked Asia's Porsche Panamera, grabbed her U-Neak handbag—which contained her handgun—slipped a hand inside, and cautiously exited the vehicle with experienced, roaming eyes. Noticing nothing out of the ordinary, she motioned to Asia, who sat slouched in the passenger seat, to exit as she walked around the front of the car.

"Good morning," a short man with a mop of carrot-colored hair and numerous freckles said while passing by.

"Morning . . ." she simply responded with a slight grin. Men were not her objective at the moment, only Asia.

"Girl, dude got swag to be a white boy," Asia commented, shutting her door. "He walk like he packing at least eight inches." She giggled lightly.

"You a mess . . ." Spandora joked back. "But no, that's not my type, boo-boo."

Together they crossed the street onto the sidewalk, eyeing the young man.

"And how you know he is packing eight inches? He caught you sleeping on the late night?"

"Oh no, boo-boo. Malik was my first and last, and besides, he can't afford me," Asia spoke like a professional gold digger.

Both women entered the salon dressed in expensive designer labels. Looking around for empty seats, Asia spotted one and casually strolled across the floor, seating herself between two young ladies who sat quietly reading from a book—Hood Consigliere by Keese. She looked around, checking her surroundings for anyone that would be a possible threat and all escape routes, just as Spandora, who sat across from her, did the same thing.

The salon was overcrowded with divas, and even though it was only a typical Thursday at Hair Estate, many of the divas sat in silence waiting their turn to get their wig done. It appeared as if everyone had been waiting for hours. Knowing she would be waiting for a while for her client to get dolled up, Spandora decided to read *Court in Da Streets* by Kevin Bullock, while others conversed or chatted on their cell phones.

A woman seated not too far from Asia began chatting to a woman seated to the left of her.

"Um, um, um." The woman shook her head. "It's crazy how that FBI chick just disappeared and can't nobody find her."

"Who you talking about, Joy?" the other replied.

"Her . . ." she responded, showing her a picture in the Herald-Sun Daily Newspaper. "It's a shame that the FBI can't even protect their own people."

"Oh yeah, I did hear about that . . . shit crazy," the next chick responded.

"As a matter of fact, I seen it on the news last night. They say they had a lead on the case, but they still haven't found a body or any witnesses," she continued, after glancing at the hood chick who had just entered the salon.

"I think I've seen her before. Didn't she go to Central?"

"Mmmmm, they say she was investigating Ceelo before he got killed and dude that used to play for Carolina."

Joy's eyebrow rose. "Which one?" Ms. Nosey asked.

"The one I pointed out to you at Tyshineak's birthday, back in the Lambo."

Suddenly remembering, Joy spoke rapidly. "Oh, I seen him out in Miami 'bout two weeks ago creeping with Pilar Sanders."

"You talking about Deion Sanders' ex? I thought she was messing with Birdman?"

Unexpectedly, like a gust of wind with hurricane speed, two masked men clad in dark jeans, Timbs, and black hoodies burst into the salon, brandishing large-caliber handguns. Everyone suddenly began screaming and attempted to scramble from their seats in search of cover.

"On the floor . . . everybody . . . now!" the first gunman barked thuggishly.

The slim U.S. Marine who had been sitting off in the corner pretending to be reading an Essence magazine quickly dropped the magazine and hustled to her feet with the incredible swiftness of an assassin. At that very moment, with blurring speed, she reached behind her back with both hands and yanked two .40-caliber federal-issued Berettas from her Fendi holsters fitted under her suit jacket. With both feet apart, she aimed at each gunman and fired.

Shots quickly exploded with ear-deafening sounds. Everyone, including the hairstylists, scrambled wildly and began screaming. A little seven-year-old girl ran in fear as the panic broke out into chaos. The two masked men aimed their weapons toward the woman, blasting shots, missing her seconds before diving to the floor, rolling in the direction of Asia, coming up on one knee, and continuing to fire. One of the gunmen got low, scrambling across the room, wildly squeezing off three quick shots with his Heckler & Koch nine-millimeter, missing the slim woman.

Asia, who had scrambled to a nearby corner, tried desperately to pull her .380 from her holster, but in a crazed state of panic, she was afraid to bolt into action due to all the shots splattering chunks of sheetrock exploding from the wall only inches above her head. She continued to scream.

A loud scream shot through the air. One of the gunmen had scooped up the little girl into his arms and stabbed the barrel of his gun against her soft temple.

"Bitch, put them hammers down," the gunman ordered. "Before I end this little girl's life."

"No!" the child's mother yelled. "Please don't hurt my baby. Please, I just buried her daddy a week ago." She cried, folding to the floor on her knees as if she were praying in church with closed hands.

Spandora stopped shooting. However, she kept both guns trained on the gunmen who held the little girl hostage. The little girl was not of concern, only Asia. She took orders from no one but Young Money. She remained silent and was now concentrating on a perfect shot—a shot that would drop her intended target without harming the little girl.

"Bitch, I said drop dem hammers!" he warned a second time. "You got five seconds or shawty dies."

Asia, sensing her bodyguard refusing to comply with the gunman's order, demanded that she lower her gun.

***

It was sometime after twelve noon when Jade called Young Money and told him that she needed to see him. The duo agreed to meet in Knightdale at 2 p.m. After ending the call with Kream, Jade paced her condo, working her brain on a way to convince Kream to sell twenty bricks of heroin to a set of Ceelo's minions. She smiled when an idea came to mind and then called Lucky back to put her second plan into effect.

Jade arrived at the spot in Knightdale around 1:58 p.m. Moments later, Kream pulled into the driveway behind Jade's Bentley. After surveying the area, Kream hopped out and climbed into Jade's car.

"Red Rum Salute," Kream stated, while adjusting his seat backward.

"Red Rum Salute . . . Look, can you touch twenty of them thangs right now?" she asked, knowing the answer to her question already.

"I can't, but I can hit speed dial and make it happen. Why, what's up?"

"Nah, I got some people that just flew in from Connecticut and they are trying to cop at least twenty."

"We can make that happen . . . when they need it?" he stated, as his phone began to ring, screaming for attention. "Talk."

Jade quickly took notice that he seemed to be fully engaged in the conversation with whomever he was conversing so aggressively with.

"What? You can't be serious . . . this can't be happening right now," he questioned.

Jade sat in silence as Kream continued to voice his opinion over the phone. "Look, you ain't gotta explain yourself. What's done is done. Let's do what we need to do to get back." He paused to listen to what was being said. "More or less, but don't move. I'm on my way," he stated before ending the call.

After explaining to Jade what was told to him over the phone, he hopped out of Jade's car into his own, burning tires as he sped off headed to meet up with Spandora and his comrades. While dancing in and out of traffic, his cell phone buzzed. "Talk."

"Yo," a familiar voice with an accent stated in a crazy way.

Recognizing the voice, he said, "Yeah, whatcha want? You got something that belongs to me?"

"I knew we both had more than just money in common. You got something that belongs to me, and I got something that belongs to you."

"I'm willing to die for mine though," Kream admitted.

"And I'll kill for mines. So listen carefully—you got sixty minutes to deliver what belongs to me or else I'll take it in blood."

"What's the price tag?"

"Two million."

"That's throwaway money . . . where can I meet you?"

"At McDonald's on Chapel Hill Blvd. Throw the money in the orange Camaro. Once the bread is counted, someone will call you with information on where to find your loved one."

"Consider it done, just don't touch her . . . see you in thirty," he responded as the phone went dead in his ear.

Malik quickly thumbed in a series of numbers and paced the device to his ear.

"Yo, Hy," he quickly spoke, "meet me at the Hair Estate right now."

Without a moment to spare, he raced through traffic like a NASCAR driver. He dipped around corners, made sharp turns, and ran damn near every stoplight he traveled through along the way. Within minutes, he spotted Snatch and Spandora standing by Snatch's Bentley. Abruptly, he stopped alongside Snatch's whip.

"Span, you good?" he asked, approaching her with a bulletproof vest over top of his all-white tee, not caring who seen him wearing it.

"Yeah, I'm good . . . just kinda mad at myself for letting them get away with Asia like that."

Hysheem pulled up, dressed in all-black fatigues, joining them.

"Shit happens to all of us at some point. We good though. I'm 'bout to go snatch this bread up real quick and meet ole buddy's peoples."

"How much bread he asking fo'?" Hysheem asked, cutting him off.

"Two mil."

"Well, let's go get that and handle that."

***

Surrounded by rapacious masked men, Asia sat with her hands bound behind her back. She had been stripped naked as a withered tree, and duct tape covered her mouth to suppress the volume of her intense voice. Even though the tape prevented her from screaming, she willfully tried yelling for help.

"Bitch, shut'cha trap before I cut yo' tongue out," one of the masked men said.

"Fam, dis bitch just got some exclusive ass head for a nigga to come off two mil so easily," Lucky said, standing over Asia's naked body.

"She worth it though," Trigger responded, as walkie-talkies sat viciously waiting for an audible voice to vocalize codes from participants who arranged such a kidnapping.

Lucky, who had been pacing the hotel room awaiting instructions, was about to go take a leak when the walkie-talkie cracked with what sounded like Zulu's voice.

"Go one . . ." he responded, pressing the button, giving his code.

"Go two . . ." the voice on the other end responded. "Kelly's in position . . . gather the insurance policy and meet me at the location we discussed last night," the voice ordered.

"Say no more. One, out," Lucky responded.

"On your feet, bitch," Trigger barked at Asia. "Just do as you're told, Shawty, and you good—you hear me?"

Asia nodded yes.

"A'ight, when my man bring the Jeep around, he gonna open the door, and when he does I want you to climb yo' naked ass in. And if you try anything, I'll kill you." He threatened.

"Lucky. Let's move out."

Asia knew without a doubt that Young Money would come through with the ransom money, and that once he paid up, the men would kill her the first chance they got. She had been held hostage at a small hotel downtown Durham and figured it would be best to resist their orders the first chance she got. What she was thinking was not a good idea, but it would provide her with a good possibility if done correctly.

So she willed away all fears and prayed for the best outcome in silence.

The moment the black SUV pulled up alongside the exit door, Trigger ordered Asia to climb into the backseat.

The moment she stepped out onto the pavement, she bolted, taking off as though she was competing in a track and field event. She spotted a couple entering the parking lot by way of a cab, and bolted again, sprinting across the parking lot barefooted in all hopes that the cab driver and its passengers would notice her and come to her rescue.

"Fuck!" Trigger cursed with a whisper, as he stood frozen, unaware of how to react. Lucky then bolted from the SUV and peered around wildly. He was about to give chase but second-guessed it the moment Asia ran smack into a parked BMW.

Asia frantically peered through the window of the BMW she had intentionally run into to gain attention. However, the driver quickly sped off. She continued to run as if she was a prisoner who had just escaped. Stepping on a piece of glass from a broken bottle, she stumbled onto the ground.

"Wo!" a voice stated, grabbing her arm by the elbow. "You alright, miss?"

Asia rolled over and locked eyes with those of the white man as if God had laid a comforting hand of protection on her. The moment he removed the tape from her mouth, she screamed in panic to use his cell phone that she quickly took notice of at his hip.

***

Kream, Hysheem, and Jade were sitting in position, eyeing the parked Camaro that sat in the parking lot of McDonald's on Chapel Hill Blvd. Behind the wheel sat a heavy-set Black woman with dreads and large-frame Dior shades, as if she was basking in the sun on some exotic island.

Kream carefully climbed from the blue Impala and rounded the back, popping the trunk. Lifting the shoulder strap of the duffel bag containing two million dollars over his head, he pulled it out of the trunk and stationed its weight on his shoulder. He then slammed the trunk closed. Quickly, he looked around and strolled over to the orange Camaro, tapping the trunk with his knuckle.

Kelly smiled and popped the trunk for him. Once he had placed the money in the trunk, closing it shut behind him, his cell phone rang. Slowly, he backed away from the car as the engine started.

"Talk," he answered.

"Baby," a voice quickly said in his ear.

"Asia, s'that you? How . . ."

"Yeah, it's me, Malik. Don't give them shit—"

"Whatchu mean?" he responded, eyeing the Camaro pulling off slowly, waiting to enter traffic.

"I got away."

Kream quickly yelled across the parking lot to Spandora, who was closer to the Camaro, to stop it, as he ran, pointing and shouting.

"Stop that bitch! Asia got away . . . stop her!" he yelled, pulling his gun free from under his arm holster.

Noticing Kream sprinting across the lot, Spandora tried making out what he shouted. Suddenly realizing what he was yelling, she steered the car into gear and stood on the gas, burning rubber. She steered directly for the Camaro and rammed into its passenger-side door with the front end of her Jeep Wrangler.

Upon feeling the impact of the charging Jeep, the Camaro rocked violently before coming to a complete stop.

"No, this bitch didn't just hit my car!" the dreaded woman yelled, trying to regain her focus.

Realizing the woman was incoherent, Spandora bolted from her Jeep. Pulling her gun from its holster, she slid across the hood of the trunk, landing on her feet like a cat, and fired a shot through the passenger-side window, killing her instantly as Snatch and Kream approached the vehicle, weapons drawn on its target.

"Good job," Hysheem said, forcing the driver-side door open. Once inside, he found the button to release the trunk lock. "Snatch, grab that bread real quick."

"Got it . . ." Snatch yelled, racing towards Jade, who had just pulled up in a rental Jeep Wrangler.

The moment the Jeep came to a halt, everyone piled in like a gang of thieves and killers. Jade slammed her foot on the gas pedal, jumping the curb, fishtailing her way into traffic before the cops could respond to such chaos. Skillfully, she managed to get away swiftly.

Three miles away from the crime scene, she pulled into a vacant lot, where they all hurriedly exited the Jeep and respectfully made way to their own personal whips, coasting off in different directions.

Once arriving home, Kream, Hysheem, and Spandora hustled inside Asia's mini-mansion to find her seated on the sofa with a well-dressed white man. Her foot appeared to be wrapped in cloth as she sat clenching a housecoat around her luscious body.

Upon seeing Kream, she sprang from the leather sofa, limping as she ran into his arms, embracing him strongly with affection. Tears ran down from her eyes as she looked over his shoulder, locking eyes with those of Spandora.

"Thank you," she whispered softly.

After she sat Kream down and explained everything to him, Young Money stood to his feet and thanked the ex-convict who made sure Asia got home safely by rewarding him with ten thousand dollars. The ex-convict thanked him in return and suggested they go into business together before shaking hands and finally leaving.

Hours later, with darkness approaching fast, Kream explained to Asia that he and Jade needed to handle some business before midnight.

"Baby, please don't go . . ." she replied. "Why can't you just wait and handle it tomorrow?"

"Asia . . ." he calmly responded. "I already gave them my word that I would do it, so it's got to go down . . . tonight. I won't be out too long. This shouldn't take any more than an hour . . . I promise." He continued while checking his vest and slipping black gloves onto his hands. "You gon' be alright, Hy and Span will be here witcha."

"Baby, I don't feel right about this," she pleaded. "After what just happened, you don't need to be out by yourself. It's a street war between you and them, but they keep losing people. This gives them every reason to get at you that much harder. At least take Hysheem with you."

For a chilling second, Young Money had a mental image of steel glinting, of blood spraying. He repressed the sign that had just been shown to him, avoiding the question. "You just don't give up, do you?"

"Nooo!" she pouted.

"Baby, in order to get from where I am to where I wanna be, I gotta make this move." He finally said, turning to leave. "Hy, make sure she don't follow me. I know how she can be at times. It's all love though." He ordered. "Angel Dust," he said, closing the door behind him.

***

High above in the cloudless sky, the full moon illuminated the parking lot of Walmart as Jade and Kream sat inconspicuously in a diamond-black Charger, engaging in conversation as they awaited the arrival of a second vehicle.

Jade pulled back her leather glove above her timepiece designer to check the time; it was almost 10:40.

"Damn!" Jade cursed, frustrated. The felons were late. "They should have been dead forty minutes ago."

"Breathe easy, Ma. Dem niggas gon' sho." Kream said, looking into Jade's eyes. "They did say they were on the way, right?"

"Yeah, but that was twenty minutes ago . . . time is of the essence."

"I feel ya, but something may have come up."

"Hell, everything is secondary when it comes to exchanging dope for dollars." There was a hint of uneasiness in Jade's voice as she gripped the steering wheel tightly with both hands. "Shit, I got a plane to catch."

"Whatever happens, gon' happen . . ." Kream responded sharply, resisting the urge to smoke a blunt as he noticed headlights from a distance reflecting in his rearview mirror. "Here comes your client now."

"Get it how you live," she reminded him in a commanding tone.

"Chill, baby girl, I got dis." He slid his leather gloves onto his tone.

He then simultaneously reached both hands into his coat pockets, positioning two concealed 9mm handguns for added protection, and thumbed both hammers back. Once he was situated, he pulled back on the door handle and exited the car, walking toward the rear where he stopped beside the trunk.

The trunk clicked open and slowly rose. Looking over into the compartment, a slight smile spread across his face as he glanced at the two dark duffel bags.

As the approaching headlights got closer, Kream swallowed the lump in his throat and suddenly found himself nervous, but the feeling gave him a great sense of power and courage. He'd never felt so free in his life, which puzzled him.

Stopping only yards away, the driver of the BMW 760 killed the lights and exited the vehicle along with his comrade. Suddenly suspicion claimed all three felons as they found themselves questioning the business arrangement and acknowledging, within a split second, they had been set up.

"What th—" Lucky yelled, reaching under his leather jacket with the instinct of a killer. Kream even-handedly stabbed both hands into his coat pockets, just as Lucky extracted a MAC-11 from under his jacket. Sensing the threat, Kream curled his fingers around the trigger of both pistols concealed within his coat jacket and immediately fired at both felons.

Kream's coat pockets exploded into fine pieces of fabric and Lucky was hit, but managed to hold down the trigger, squeezing off a short burst of continuous shots, catching Kream in the chest with the slugs as bullets tore into his body, knocking him to the concrete.

Kream struggled to remain standing on his feet as he desperately braced himself using the open trunk as a crutch. He jerked violently as two additional bullets ripped through his body, exiting his back.

"Fuck!" he grunted between clenched teeth as he raised his gun and pulled back on the trigger, then dropped to the ground, dying.

He slid to the pavement, grunting in pain. He couldn't believe Jade had set them all up. "But why?" he questioned himself as he slowly began slipping in and out of consciousness.

Hearing a faint voice calling his name, Kream struggled to lift his head in Jade's direction.

"Why?" he asked softly before losing consciousness again.

Jade smiled surreptitiously as she looked down over Young Money's body. "Why? . . . I'ma mirror. What you see is what you reflect. So if you see something wrong with me, you did it." She then closed the trunk and walked over to the second car and looked into the backseat. Spotting a duffel bag, Jade reached into the car and pulled out the duffel, slung it over her shoulder by the strap as she looked down at the corpses of both Trigger and Lucky.

Silently, she climbed back into the rented Charger and drove off into the night with twenty kilos of heroin and stacks of dead presidents.

Chapter 15

"Has Mr. Carter Awakened Yet?"
-Agent Kimbro-

Asia sat alongside Kream while holding his hand as he lay motionless in a Duke hospital bed. He had fallen into a deep coma after nearly being shot to death. For the past three weeks, she refused to leave his side, except to get a bite to eat, shower, or change clothes.

"Asia, I think you should go home and get some rest," Spandora said while standing on the opposite side of Malik's bed. "He knows you're here, and if I know him like I do, he's fighting like hell to come back to you. You do want to look fabulous for him when God decides to open his eyes, don't you? What I suggest is that you go home, get some rest, and come back and visit him later . . . go on, I'll be here. He'll be fine until you get back."

Asia knew she was right, and standing by his bedside wouldn't help any. It was all up to him to fight his way out of his current situation. She wanted so desperately to see his eyes open so she could soon take him home. Standing to her feet, she looked down on him, scrutinizing the wires and tubes snaking from his body under the bed sheets, attached to a variety of different machines. She kissed him on the cheek.

"Will you call me when he wakes up?"

"Sure," Spandora replied.

Asia turned on her heel to face Spandora. "Do me a favor, Asia," Spandora said.

"Anything."

"Will you call Hysheem when you get downstairs and let him know that I won't be home until later?"

"Sure, as soon as I get to the car." Asia smiled. "So have you two decided on a wedding day yet?" she asked, eyeing the fifty-thousand-dollar engagement ring Hysheem had given her as a gift two days ago, during a Hornets versus Knicks game in Charlotte.

"Yes, we have . . ." She suddenly stopped talking. Her eyes grew extremely large.

Asia noticed the look on Spandora's face and asked, "What's wrong?"

"I thought I just seen his finger move, Asia . . ." she whispered. "I swear to God his finger moved."

The second Asia turned to face Kream, three FBI agents entered the room, dressed in dark blue suits. They looked about and around the room as if inspecting for more evidence.

"Has Mr. Carter awakened yet?" Agent Kimbro asked.

"Not yet," Asia whispered, lightly turning back towards Kream, knowing the agents would continue to visit until he did wake up so they could question him.

Asia suddenly gasped and cupped her mouth with both hands. "His eyes are open, Spandora."

Kream lay motionless in bed with eyes roaming and scanning the room as if he had no clue where he was. Everyone in the room stared down at him in silence. Spandora left the room only to return seconds later with two nurses and a doctor.

"Malik, can you hear me?" one of the nurses asked politely. Upon receiving no response, she began carefully checking his vital signs and listening to his heartbeat, which pumped normally. "Malik, can you feel my hand?" Still no response.

Asia affectionately moved closer to his bedside and took his hand in hers with tears in her eyes. "Baby, I miss you so much."

His lips twitched before speaking. "Who are you . . . what . . . why . . . why am I here?" he mumbled.

"No! What's wrong with him? Why doesn't he remember me?"

The nurses tried to escort her out of the room, but she resisted with a will so strong and powerful, it could be nothing but love. One of the doctors who had been examining Kream's progress slowly explained to Asia that Malik may be suffering from loss of memory, and that sometimes when patients slip into a coma, they lose the power to recall or remember things. He explained that Kream may have been diagnosed with amnesia.

Asia was speechless. She didn't know what to say or think. "Will he ever be back to his normal self?" she asked.

"It's too early to say at the present moment. We'll just have to wait and see. It could be a day or many years before he remembers all that he had forgotten. We'll know more after we run a series of tests on him."

"Oh my God . . ." Asia nervously said.

After running more tests, the doctors left the room so that Asia and Spandora could spend more private time with him. The moment the nurses and doctors left the room, Mr. Kimbro attempted to drill Kream with a string of questions. However, he just stared at them in silence as his companions continuously informed them that he was in critical condition and no longer remembered past or present events.

Asia, in return, drilled the agents after one of them admitted mistakenly they had nothing on him visually but knew he was a dope boy.

"If that's the case, then you have nothing . . ." Asia said. "So I suggest you all leave and not return until you have strong assets to start an investigation. Furthermore, attempting to question a patient before a full recovery is considered harassment. So please leave before I file a lawsuit on all three of y'all." She argued as if she stood outside of a courthouse after a big case.

"Now that's how you protect your man and his rights." Spandora smiled, high-fiving Asia once the agents left.

"Gurl, I'm so sick of them unjust bastards," she responded, turning to face Kream with sadness in her eyes. "I just want him to remember who I am," she cried.

Kream hadn't really spoken much while others stopped by to visit, but noticing his angel crying touched him in a way he had no choice but to verbalize his true feelings toward Asia. "Baby, don't cry," he surprisingly said. "It's gon' take more than two slugs to get rid of me, Y.M.," he swore, smiling with a dry mouth.

"Baby, you had me scared to death . . ." she cried. "I love you so much, Malik."

"I love you more, Asia." He paused. "And just so you'll know, I don't have amnesia. I heard everything that was said to me or around me."

Asia couldn't believe Malik had heard everything that was said around him, so she filled him in on all that transpired during his time of recovery. She revealed to him that the night he left, she somehow talked Hysheem into following him the night he got shot. She also explained how Snatch kicked in Jade's door and shot and killed her. Then, two days later, after a night of partying, Zulu and Rachel went to a late dinner at a restaurant in downtown Raleigh, unaware he'd been spotted by a young thug trying to make his bones with Hysheem. The thug ran up the block to a Chinese takeout joint where four members of ZooGang were eating and told them he'd just spotted Zulu. In a hot second, all four members dropped their egg rolls, picked up their guns, and phoned Hysheem, who ordered the hit. However, when they pulled in front of the Chinese spot, Zulu and his companion were long gone.

Kream couldn't believe how much had transpired in the three-week period he had been hospitalized. But he knew his life was endangered as long as Zulu existed.

"Baby, I know you don't want to hear this, but I gotta find dude before he finds us . . . in life, one must face the consequences of his actions to become the man he's trying to become . . . so I gotta do what I gotta do before he do me . . ."

"I know, baby," she simply whispered. "Just be careful, 'cause you have a Kream on the way."

TO BE CONTINUED…

Lock Down Publications and Ca$h Presents
Assisted Publishing Packages

Due to an increase in the price of services we have increased our prices. The prices below reflect the price increase as of 11/1/24.

BASIC PACKAGE	UPGRADED PACKAGE
$699 Editing Cover Design Formatting	**$1000** Typing Editing Cover Design Formatting Upload eBooks to Amazon Upload Paperback to Amazon
ADVANCE PACKAGE	LDP SUPREME PACKAGE
$1,400 Typing Editing (line editing/content) Cover Design Formatting Copyright Registration Proofreading Upload eBooks to Amazon Upload Paperback to Amazon	**$1,700** Typing Editing (line editing/content) Cover Design Formatting Copyright Registration Proofreading Set up Amazon Account Upload eBooks to Amazon Upload Paperback to Amazon Advertise on LDP's Amazon and Facebook Page

***

Other services available upon request.
Additional charges may apply

Lock Down Publications
P.O. Box 944
Stockbridge, GA 30281-9998
Phone: 470 303-9761
Email: lockdownpublications@gmail.com

Submission Guideline

Submit the first three chapters of your completed manuscript to ldpsubmissions@gmail.com. In the subject line add **Your Book's Title**. The manuscript must be in a Word Doc file and sent as an attachment. Document should be in Times New Roman, double spaced, and in size 12 font. Also, provide your synopsis and full contact information. If sending multiple submissions, they must each be in a separate email.

Have a story but no way to send it electronically? You can still submit to LDP/Ca$h Presents. Send in the first three chapters, written or typed, of your completed manuscript to:

LDP: Submissions Dept
P.O. Box 944
Stockbridge, GA 30281-9998

DO NOT send original manuscript. Must be a duplicate.
Provide your synopsis and a cover letter containing your full contact information.

Thanks for considering LDP and Ca$h Presents.

NEW RELEASES

BLOODLINE OF A SAVAGE 1-3
THESE VICIOUS STREETS 1-3
RELENTLESS GOON 1-3
BY PRINCE A. TAUHID

THE BUTTERFLY MAFIA 1-3
BY FUMIYA PAYNE

A THUG'S STREET PRINCESS 1&2
BY MEESHA

CITY OF SMOKE 3
BY MOLOTTI

GET IT IN SLUGS 1 &2
BY B. STALL

STANDING ON HER BUSINESS 1&2
BY DG SANTANA

STEPPERS 1,2&3
THE REAL BADDIES OF CHI-RAQ
BY KING RIO

THE LANE 1&2
BY KEN-KEN SPENCE

THUG OF SPADES 1&2
LOVE IN THE TRENCHES 2
CORNER BOYS
BY COREY ROBINSON

TIL DEATH 3
BY ARYANNA

THE BIRTH OF A GANGSTER 4
BY DELMONT PLAYER

PRODUCT OF THE STREETS 1-3
BY DEMOND "MONEY" ANDERSON

NO TIME FOR ERROR
BY KEESE

MONEY HUNGRY DEMONS 1-2
BY TRANAY ADAMS

HUB CITY MENACE 1-3
BY J. WHITE

A THUGGISH PASSION 1&2
LAND OF DA HOOLIGANZ 1-4
KILLAZ ON STANDBY 1&2
BY IRA B.

FO'EVA ROLLIN 1&2
BY ASSA RAYMOND BAKER

THE LEVEL UP 1&3
BY LUXURY KING

Coming Soon from Lock Down Publications/Ca$h Presents

IF YOU CROSS ME ONCE 6
ANGEL V
By Anthony Fields

A THUGS STREET PRINCESS 3
By Meesha

CORNER BOYS 2
By Corey Robinson

THA TAKEOVER
By Keith Chandler

BETRAYAL OF A G 2
By Ray Vinci

SAVAGE FAMILY EMPIRE 1&2
SOULLESS GOON 1,2&3
THE DIRTY SIDE OF MONEY 1,2&3
By Prince

FOR MY ENEMY'S SAKE
AMBITIONS OF A SLIDER
FRESH OFF DA PORCH
By IRA B.

THE TRUCKLOAD 1-4
TIPPIN' THE SCALES 1-3
BAD BITCHES WIT GUNZ 3
PROBLEM SOLVED 2
By Christopher "Diesel" Hornezes

Available Now

RESTRAINING ORDER 1 & 2
By **CA$H & Coffee**

LOVE KNOWS NO BOUNDARIES 1-3
By **Coffee**

RAISED AS A GOON I, II, III & IV
BRED BY THE SLUMS I, II, III
BLAST FOR ME I & II
ROTTEN TO THE CORE I II III
A BRONX TALE I, II, III
DUFFLE BAG CARTEL I II III IV V VI
HEARTLESS GOON I II III IV V
A SAVAGE DOPEBOY I II
DRUG LORDS I II III
CUTTHROAT MAFIA I II
KING OF THE TRENCHES
By **Ghost**

LAY IT DOWN I & II
LAST OF A DYING BREED I II
BLOOD STAINS OF A SHOTTA I & II III
By **Jamaica**

LOYAL TO THE GAME I II III
LIFE OF SIN I, II III
By **TJ & Jelissa**

IF LOVING HIM IS WRONG…I & II
LOVE ME EVEN WHEN IT HURTS I II III
By **Jelissa**

PUSH IT TO THE LIMIT
By **Bre' Hayes**

BLOODY COMMAS I & II
SKI MASK CARTEL I, II & III
KING OF NEW YORK I II, III IV V
RISE TO POWER I II III
COKE KINGS I II III IV V
BORN HEARTLESS I II III IV
KING OF THE TRAP I II
By **T.J. Edwards**

WHEN THE STREETS CLAP BACK I & II III
THE HEART OF A SAVAGE I II III IV
MONEY MAFIA I II
LOYAL TO THE SOIL I II III
By **Jibril Williams**

A DISTINGUISHED THUG STOLE MY HEART I II & III
LOVE SHOULDN'T HURT I II III IV
RENEGADE BOYS 1-4
PAID IN KARMA 1-3
SAVAGE STORMS 1-3
AN UNFORESEEN LOVE 1-3
BABY, I'M WINTERTIME COLD 1-3
A THUG'S STREET PRINCESS 1&2
By **Meesha**

A GANGSTER'S CODE 1-3
A GANGSTER'S SYN 1-3
THE SAVAGE LIFE 1-3
CHAINED TO THE STREETS 1-3
BLOOD ON THE MONEY 1-3
A GANGSTA'S PAIN 1-3
BEAUTIFUL LIES AND UGLY TRUTHS
CHURCH IN THESE STREETS
By **J-Blunt**

CUM FOR ME 1-8
An LDP Erotica Collaboration

BLOOD OF A BOSS 1-5
SHADOWS OF THE GAME
TRAP BASTARD
By **Askari**

THE STREETS BLEED MURDER 1-3
THE HEART OF A GANGSTA 1-3
By **Jerry Jackson**

WHEN A GOOD GIRL GOES BAD
By **Adrienne**

THE COST OF LOYALTY 1-3
By **Kweli**

BRIDE OF A HUSTLA 1-3
THE FETTI GIRLS 1-3
CORRUPTED BY A GANGSTA 1-4
BLINDED BY HIS LOVE
THE PRICE YOU PAY FOR LOVE 1-3
DOPE GIRL MAGIC 1-3
By **Destiny Skai**

A KINGPIN'S AMBITION
A KINGPIN'S AMBITION II
I MURDER FOR THE DOUGH
By **Ambitious**

TRUE SAVAGE 1-7
DOPE BOY MAGIC 1-3
MIDNIGHT CARTEL 1-3
CITY OF KINGZ 1&2
NIGHTMARE ON SILENT AVE
THE PLUG OF LIL MEXICO 1&2
CLASSIC CITY
By **Chris Green**

A GANGSTER'S REVENGE 1-4
THE BOSS MAN'S DAUGHTERS 1-5
A SAVAGE LOVE 1&2
BAE BELONGS TO ME 1&2
A HUSTLER'S DECEIT 1-3
WHAT BAD BITCHES DO 1-3
SOUL OF A MONSTER 1-3
KILL ZONE
A DOPE BOY'S QUEEN 1-3
TIL DEATH 1-3
IMMA DIE BOUT MINE 1-6
DYING FOR LIKES
By **Aryanna**

A DOPEBOY'S PRAYER
By **Eddie "Wolf" Lee**

THE KING CARTEL 1-3
By **Frank Gresham**

THESE NIGGAS AIN'T LOYAL 1-3
By **Nikki Tee**

GANGSTA SHYT 1-3
By **CATO**

THE ULTIMATE BETRAYAL
By **Phoenix**

BOSS'N UP 1-3
By **Royal Nicole**

I LOVE YOU TO DEATH
By **Destiny J**

I RIDE FOR MY HITTA
I STILL RIDE FOR MY HITTA
By **Misty Holt**

LOVE & CHASIN' PAPER
By **Qay Crockett**

TO DIE IN VAIN
SINS OF A HUSTLA
By **ASAD**

BROOKLYN HUSTLAZ
By **Boogsy Morina**

BROOKLYN ON LOCK 1 & 2
By **Sonovia**

GANGSTA CITY
By **Teddy Duke**

A DRUG KING AND HIS DIAMOND 1-3
A DOPEMAN'S RICHES
HER MAN, MINE'S TOO 1&2
CASH MONEY HO'S
THE WIFEY I USED TO BE 1&2
PRETTY GIRLS DO NASTY THINGS
By **Nicole Goosby**

LIPSTICK KILLAH 1-3
CRIME OF PASSION 1-3
FRIEND OR FOE 1-3
By **Mimi**

TRAPHOUSE KING 1-3
KINGPIN KILLAZ 1-3
STREET KINGS 1&2
PAID IN BLOOD 1&2
CARTEL KILLAZ 1-3
DOPE GODS 1&2
By **Hood Rich**

THE STREETS ARE CALLING
By **Duquie Wilson**

STEADY MOBBN' 1-3
THE STREETS STAINED MY SOUL 1-3
By **Marcellus Allen**

WHO SHOT YA 1-3
SON OF A DOPE FIEND 1-4
HEAVEN GOT A GHETTO 1&2
SKI MASK MONEY 1&2
By **Renta**

GORILLAZ IN THE BAY 1-4
TEARS OF A GANGSTA 1/&2
3X KRAZY 1&2
STRAIGHT BEAST MODE 1&2
By **DE'KARI**

TRIGGADALE 1-3
MURDA WAS THE CASE 1-3
By **Elijah R. Freeman**

SLAUGHTER GANG 1-3
RUTHLESS HEART 1-3
By **Willie Slaughter**

GOD BLESS THE TRAPPERS 1-3
THESE SCANDALOUS STREETS 1-3
FEAR MY GANGSTA 1-5
THESE STREETS DON'T LOVE NOBODY 1-2
BURY ME A G 1-5
A GANGSTA'S EMPIRE 1-4
THE DOPEMAN'S BODYGAURD 1&2
THE REALEST KILLAZ 1-3
THE LAST OF THE OGS 1-3
By **Tranay Adams**

MARRIED TO A BOSS 1-3
By **Destiny Skai & Chris Green**

KINGZ OF THE GAME 1-7
CRIME BOSS 1-4
By **Playa Ray**

FUK SHYT
By **Blakk Diamond**

DON'T F#CK WITH MY HEART 1&2
By **Linnea**

ADDICTED TO THE DRAMA 1-3
IN THE ARM OF HIS BOSS
By **Jamila**

LOYALTY AIN'T PROMISED 1&2
By **Keith Williams**

YAYO 1-4
A SHOOTER'S AMBITION 1&2
BRED IN THE GAME
By **S. Allen**

TRAP GOD 1-3
RICH $AVAGE 1-3
MONEY IN THE GRAVE 1-3
CARTEL MONEY 1&2
By **Martell Troublesome Bolden**

FOREVER GANGSTA 1&2
GLOCKS ON SATIN SHEETS 1&2
By **Adrian Dulan**

TOE TAGZ 1-4
LEVELS TO THIS SHYT 1&2
IT'S JUST ME AND YOU
By **Ah'Million**

KINGPIN DREAMS 1-3
RAN OFF ON DA PLUG
By **Paper Boi Rari**

THE STREETS MADE ME 1-3
By **Larry D. Wright**

CONFESSIONS OF A GANGSTA 1-4
CONFESSIONS OF A JACKBOY 1-3
CONFESSIONS OF A HITMAN
CONFESSIONS OF A DOPE BOY
By **Nicholas Lock**

I'M NOTHING WITHOUT HIS LOVE
SINS OF A THUG
TO THE THUG I LOVED BEFORE
A GANGSTA SAVED XMAS
IN A HUSTLER I TRUST
By **Monet Dragun**

QUIET MONEY 1-3
THUG LIFE 1-3
EXTENDED CLIP 1&2
A GANGSTA'S PARADISE
By **Trai'Quan**

CAUGHT UP IN THE LIFE 1-3
THE STREETS NEVER LET GO 1-3
By **Robert Baptiste**

NEW TO THE GAME 1-3
MONEY, MURDER & MEMORIES 1-3
By **Malik D. Rice**

CREAM 2-3
THE STREETS WILL TALK
By **Yolanda Moore**

THE STREETS WILL NEVER CLOSE 1-3
By **K'ajji**

LIFE OF A SAVAGE 1-4
A GANGSTA'S QUR'AN 1-4
MURDA SEASON 1-3
GANGLAND CARTEL 1-3
CHI'RAQ GANGSTAS 1-4
KILLERS ON ELM STREET 1-3
JACK BOYZ N DA BRONX 1-3
A DOPEBOY'S DREAM 1-3
JACK BOYS VS DOPE BOYS 1-3
COKE GIRLZ
COKE BOYS
SOSA GANG 1&2
BRONX SAVAGES
BODYMORE KINGPINS
BLOOD OF A GOON
By **Romell Tukes**

CONCRETE KILLA 1-3
VICIOUS LOYALTY 1-3
BLOODY MONEY BAGS
By **Kingpen**

THE ULTIMATE SACRIFICE 1-6
KHADIFI
IF YOU CROSS ME ONCE 1-3
ANGEL 1-4
IN THE BLINK OF AN EYE
By **Anthony Fields**

THE LIFE OF A HOOD STAR
By **Ca$h & Rashia Wilson**

NIGHTMARES OF A HUSTLA 1-3
BLOOD AND GAMES 1&2
By **King Dream**

GHOST MOB
By **Stilloan Robinson**

HARD AND RUTHLESS 1&2
MOB TOWN 251
THE BILLIONAIRE BENTLEYS 1-3
REAL G'S MOVE IN SILENCE
By **Von Diesel**

MOB TIES 1-7
SOUL OF A HUSTLER, HEART OF A KILLER 1-3
GORILLAZ IN THE TRENCHES
OOPS CRY TOO 1&2
THE DAUGHTER OF A CARTEL BOSS
By **SayNoMore**

BODYMORE MURDERLAND 1-3
THE BIRTH OF A GANGSTER 1-4
By **Delmont Player**

FOR THE LOVE OF A BOSS 1&2
By **C. D. Blue**

KILLA KOUNTY 1-5
TENDER
By **Khufu**

MOBBED UP 1-4
THE BRICK MAN 1-5
THE COCAINE PRINCESS 1-10
STEPPERS 1-3
SUPER GREMLIN 1-4
A GANGSTA'S SON
By **King Rio**

MONEY GAME 1&2
By **Smoove Dolla**

A GANGSTA'S KARMA 1-5
By **FLAME**

KING OF THE TRENCHES 1-3
By **GHOST & TRANAY ADAMS**

BAD BITCHES WIT GUNZ 1&2
PROBLEM SOLVED
By "Christopher Diesel" Hornezes

QUEEN OF THE ZOO 1&2
By **Black Migo**

GRIMEY WAYS 1-3
BETRAYAL OF A G
By **Ray Vinci**

XMAS WITH AN ATL SHOOTER
By **Ca$h & Destiny Skai**

KING KILLA 1&2
By **Vincent "Vitto" Holloway**

BETRAYAL OF A THUG 1&2
By **Fre$h**

COUNTDOWN OF A KILLA 1&2
SEX, MURDER AND GOD 1&2
GUNS DOWN, BOTTOMS UP 1&2
By Lo-Life

THE MURDER QUEENS 1-7
By **Michael Gallon**

FOR THE LOVE OF BLOOD 1-4
By **Jamel Mitchell**

NO TIME FOR ERROR 2 | KEESE

HOOD CONSIGLIERE 1&2
NO TIME FOR ERROR
By **Keese**

PROTÉGÉ OF A LEGEND 1,2&3
LOVE IN THE TRENCHES 1&2
By **Corey Robinson**

THE PLUG'S RUTHLESS DAUGHTER 1&2
By **Tony Daniels**

BORN IN THE GRAVE 1-3
CRIME PAYS
By **Self Made Tay**

MOAN IN MY MOUTH
By **XTASY**

TORN BETWEEN A GANGSTER AND A GENTLEMAN
By **J-BLUNT & Miss Kim**

LOYALTY IS EVERYTHING 1-3
CITY OF SMOKE 1-3
By **Molotti**

HERE TODAY GONE TOMORROW 1&2
By **Fly Rock**

WOMEN LIE MEN LIE 1-4
FIFTY SHADES OF SNOW 1-3
STACK BEFORE YOU SPLURGE
GIRLS FALL LIKE DOMINOES
NAÏVE TO THE STREETS
By **ROY MILLIGAN**

PILLOW PRINCESS
By **S. Hawkins**

THE BUTTERFLY MAFIA 1-3
SALUTE MY SAVAGERY 1&2
By **Fumiya Payne**

THE LANE 1&2
By Ken-Ken Spence

THE PUSSY TRAP 1-5
By **Nene Capri**

DIRTY DNA
By **Blaque**

SANCTIFIED AND HORNY
by **XTASY**

BOOKS BY LDP'S CEO, CA$H

TRUST IN NO MAN
TRUST IN NO MAN 2
TRUST IN NO MAN 3
BONDED BY BLOOD
SHORTY GOT A THUG
THUGS CRY
THUGS CRY 2
THUGS CRY 3
TRUST NO BITCH
TRUST NO BITCH 2
TRUST NO BITCH 3
TIL MY CASKET DROPS
RESTRAINING ORDER
RESTRAINING ORDER 2
IN LOVE WITH A CONVICT
LIFE OF A HOOD STAR
XMAS WITH AN ATL SHOOTER

www.ingramcontent.com/pod-product-compliance
Lightning Source LLC
Chambersburg PA
CBHW070519260626
47161CB00004B/1593